OUT OF THE WAR

FRANCIS WYNDHAM

Out of the War

DUCKWORTH

First published in 1974 by
Gerald Duckworth & Co. Ltd
The Old Piano Factory
43 Gloucester Crescent, London NW1

ISBN 0 7156 0866 5

Printed in Great Britain by
Bristol Typesetting Co. Ltd.
Barton Manor - St. Philips
Bristol

Contents

Preface

These stories were written between the ages of 17 and 20, from 1942 to 1945, while I was hanging about waiting to be called up and while I was convalescing after I had been invalided out of the army. I believe I made tentative efforts to get them published, but cannot recall any details beyond the fact that all were unsuccessful: my collection of rejection slips has not survived. Indeed, I thought that I had destroyed the manuscripts as well until I came upon them not long ago, while I was preparing to move house, hidden at the back of a drawer. Enough time had elapsed for me to be able to read them, if not with complete detachment, at least with a minimum of self-consciousness. They seemed to have been written by someone else – and, in a sense, I suppose they were.

Lately, I have been trying to remember things which for thirty years I had been trying to forget. The war was a tragic time for most people, exciting perhaps for some: for me, an adolescent when it began and a delayed adolescent when it ended, it was a period of stagnation. Uncertainty and inaction are negative ills of which one cannot bear to be reminded until a long time later, when even the depressing contours of frustration may be softened by nostalgia. Many people pass their adolescence in an emotional void, waiting for something – anything – to happen, and wondering with increasing desperation if it ever will. In wartime, everyone not directly involved with the fighting found themselves in a similar state of suspension. I now see that this condition gave my stories a unifying theme, although I was unaware of it when I wrote them. Their desolate cinema-cafés, dirty milk-bars and dimly-lit station-buffets evoke for me not only my own frame of mind at that time, but a mood which was then more widely shared than I had realised. For this reason, I am less embarrassed by them than I had expected to be.

vii

The rejection slips had almost convinced me that I would never make a writer – the one thing I wanted to be. None the less, the story called 'Davenant Road' was published in 1946 in the *New Savoy*, a periodical whose first and last issue was edited by Mara Meulen and myself. Raymond Mortimer of the *New Statesman* and Alan Pryce-Jones of the *Times Literary Supplement* liked it enough to give me work as a reviewer. My own life seemed to start up again, together with the post-war world : the stories had belonged to an interim. From then on, I confined myself to various forms of journalism. When I rediscovered them in 1972, I showed them to Karl Miller, who had recently asked me if I had ever tried to write fiction. He published 'Punctuality' in the *Listener* : an encouraging gesture which has led to the belated appearance of this book.

I remember that 'Saturday' was the earliest story to be written, and 'Sunday' the second. The hospital described in 'Out of the War' (the only straightforwardly autobiographical piece in the collection) was the first of several in which my brief career as a soldier was passed. Enforced passivity sometimes stimulates invention, and it was here that I started 'Davenant Road', followed by the other stories about lonely girls whose socially limited predicaments I imagined as a metaphor for my own physically restricted situation. I am sure that they all eventually joined the Women's Services (Edna the ATS, Agatha the WAAF and Iris the WRNS) and I hope they had a good war.

Francis Wyndham,
Boxing Day, 1973

Out of the War

IT was about six o'clock in the evening when I was brought into the orthopaedic ward. The two girls in the ATS who had taken it in turns to drive the ambulance carried me in on a stretcher, which they laid down on the floor, so that the room seemed very big to me, and the ceiling very high. The girls did not know what to do next, and whispered together uneasily. At length one went to fetch my papers, which had been left in the ambulance, and the other disappeared in search of a nurse.

The walls of the ward were white; so were the bedspreads and the patients' faces and their huge bandaged limbs suspended a few inches from the beds. As it was evening, all these things seemed grey, and there appeared to be a light grey mist filling the room. Nobody spoke or moved while I lay on the floor. The ten patients sat still, propped up by many pillows, and some had the black earphones which hung behind each bed clamped to their ears. These had an abstracted air, but the wireless programme, inaudible to me, seemed not to prevent them from reading their magazines, and, turning a page of *Picture Post* or *Everybody's*, one would lift his head for a moment to attend to the broadcast buzzing at his ears; then, no longer seeking meaning in the noise, transfer his mind to the printed page lying on the white counterpane.

Not far from me a man stood upright. His body from the waist to the neck was encased in smooth plaster of paris, and one of his arms was supported at an angle, shoulder-level. He had the look of an enamel model in a draper's window or a cardboard advertisement propped upright in a cinema foyer. When he blinked, or turned his head, the effect was therefore rather sinister.

A wardmaid came into the room. I knew that she was a wardmaid because of the dinginess of her dress; her halo-like cap was on askew at the back of her head. She bent over me a kind, intelligent face; then she looked at the man who was standing, and, moving her lips with care, she uttered a strange babbling noise, a string of vowel sounds slightly distorted by a gurgle in her throat, as though there were a bubble there, continually bursting and re-forming. I learnt for certain later, what I guessed then, that many of the wardmaids at the hospital were patients who were deaf and dumb.

The ambulance driver came back with a tall nurse (from where I lay she looked a giantess) who approached the wardmaid and shouted into her ear, 'You'll find Sister in her office, Elsie.' Elsie went away and the nurse and the drivers helped me into bed (for the other driver had returned, munching a biscuit bought at a Church Army mobile canteen which stood at the hospital entrance.) I was to know that this nurse was called Nurse Bennett. She had a long freckled face, and crinkly sandy hair. Always smiling and humming to herself, she was brisk, efficient and good-humoured.

One of the drivers, a fat, dark girl, said 'Cheerio, laddie,' and went away with her friend. I knew that they were bound for a restaurant opposite, where they would drink some tea, as they had arranged this on the way to the hospital, and I wished that I could go with them.

The ward was divided by a partition built across it which had an open space in the middle for the aisle to run through. I was next to the partition, which was as high as the bed; above it there was a curtain which, when drawn, separated one set of six beds from the other – each division consisting of three beds against the two opposite walls. Nurse Bennett had drawn this curtain, cutting me off from one half of the room, with some idea that I might prefer the semi-privacy it afforded while the stretcher was lifted to the level of the bed and while I rolled off it, on to the rubber ring which had been placed beneath the sheet.

'All right, old chap?' she asked.

'Yes, thank you.'

'Good man.'

She strode away, leaving the curtain still drawn. I lay back on the pillows and the feeling of sickness caused by the jolting ambulance drive began to pass away. I was conscious of a muttering noise just above my head; this came from my earphones, which stuttered away distantly and maddeningly, only to assume volume and coherence when actually over my ears.

A red-haired man, evidently a soldier, looked up from his magazine.

'She sang that well,' he said appreciatively, and I gathered that an invisible crooner had that moment finished her song.

It was then that the curtain beside me began to twitch. I understood that the man in the bed beyond it was trying to draw it. I saw a hairy hand with a ring on one finger jerking it back nervously, but the hand could only draw the curtain half-way and its owner remained invisible to me. I drew the curtain all the way back. In the bed next to mine a dark-haired man of about fifty was smiling at me. Both his legs were supported by a kind of pulley so that they should not touch the bed.

'I don't like to have the curtain drawn like that,' he said. 'I can't see what's going on. But they're always drawing it. It cuts me off from half the room and I like to see what's going on.'

Almost at once he told me his story, the reason for his presence in the hospital. He told it in an unemotional voice, not at all the sort of voice usually used to describe catastrophes, and while doing so he continued to smile his nervous smile, baring uneven teeth in a haggard face.

He was a postman in the town, a widower with an only son, a boy of fifteen. They had been walking together one evening, returning home from a public house, when an army lorry which was passing had swerved into the side of the road and run them over. This was some months ago. His legs and arms had been badly injured, but he was now doing surprisingly well, and although it had at first been predicted that he would be crippled for life, it seemed likely that he would make a complete recovery. His son had lain in the bed on the other side of mine. The doctors had operated on the boy, taking off both his legs, without asking his father's consent. Shortly after that the boy had died. The postman repeated, 'It was very wrong of them not to ask my permission. I was very poorly then and perhaps they didn't want to worry me, but they should have told me they were going to take off his legs.'

It seemed that the shock of the discovery of this operation had been so great that it still outweighed in the postman's mind that of his son's subsequent death.

I offered him a packet of cigarettes, of which I had a store,

3

because it appeared that he had no money at all in the world, and depended entirely on his friends who came to see him every visitor's day. He refused them, and seemed rather embarrassed. A few minutes later he in his turn offered me a biscuit, saying 'My neighbour brought me these yesterday. She's very good to me.' I refused, and he seemed satisfied; I understood that it worried him to borrow from someone whom he would think it necessary somehow to pay back.

He repeated his story to me the next morning, and after that every morning and evening. Whenever my curtain had been drawn to screen me while I washed, used the bedpan, or was visited by a doctor, I could sense his uneasiness on the other side of it. The nurses never remembered to draw it back. When whatever private activity I had been engaged on was over, there would be a short time of suspense; then the hand would start its ineffectual twitching. The curtain drawn, he would smile apologetically.

'I hate to be cut off like that. I like to see what's going on.'

Shortly after my arrival in the ward, another stretcher was brought in, and the patient deposited on the bed next to mine, which had till then been empty. At first it seemed that the newcomer was a young man, probably a soldier; but when the time for the evening wash came, and he took off his pyjama jacket and sat up in bed, the thinness of his arms and the whiteness of his chest showed that he could not be more than fourteen. This pleased the postman.

'It's funny,' he said. 'There always seems to be a lad in that bed. That was the bed my boy was in, and after him there was another lad of fifteen. He was a nice boy, he left before you came. Now there's another laddie.'

He leant forward and smiled at the boy, and would have liked to have spoken to him, only my presence between them made this difficult. He did shout a remark, but the boy did not know it was meant for him, although several of the other patients looked up.

I soon found that the only nurse who made any impression on the ward was Nurse Bennett, the tall one with red hair. She was always addressed as Nurse Bennett, while the others were merely known as 'nurse'. She was very friendly with the patients, who loved to tease her. One day the red-haired soldier called her as she passed his bed.

4

'Nurse Bennett.'

'Yes, Ginger?'

'I want to ask you something.'

'Well, buck up about it, because I'm busy.'

'It says in the Bible that Adam and Eve were the first people on the earth, doesn't it?'

'Yes,' said Nurse Bennett guardedly.

'And they had two sons, Cain and Abel, didn't they?'

'Yes.'

'Cain killed Abel, is that right?'

'Yes, Ginger.'

'Then Cain went off somewhere and got married. Who,' Ginger asked triumphantly, 'did he marry?'

Nurse Bennett pulled a face. 'You've got me there, I'm afraid, Ginge. But I think I can explain. You see, we're not supposed to take the Bible too literally. It describes things how they probably did happen, but it can't know for certain, and all it says isn't strictly true. But it is true, though not always absolutely true. Do you see?'

'I see, Nurse Bennett,' said Ginger, grinning and winking at the other patients.

'Now I want to ask *you* something,' said the nurse. 'Adam and Eve and pinchme . . .' but she was interrupted by Ginger who pinched her arm. She gave a little shriek, then walked off smiling; her voice could be heard shouting orders to a nurse in the passage.

The red-haired soldier would often tell Nurse Bennett coarse jokes, to see how she would react. She never laughed at these, but continued to smile indulgently, only saying, 'I think you're revolting,' or, 'I'm surprised at you, Ginge. You wouldn't talk like that to your mother, now would you?' Ginger would say of her when she was out of the rom, 'She's a caution, that Nurse Bennett. She's got red hair like me, we're a pair. We get along all right.'

There was one subject about which the ward liked to tease Nurse Bennett, which offended her and made her cross. She was the captain of a hockey team made up by the nurses at the hospital. She took this very seriously. Before a match, there would be an atmosphere of restrained excitement in the ward. Nurses, while washing patients, would talk about the game to each other over their bodies. 'My dear, I haven't played for *years*. Not since school . . .' After the match, Ginger would say to Nurse Bennett, 'Who won?'

'They did.' The opposite team was that of the Technical College in the town.

'How many goals did you score, then?'

'I didn't score any. I nearly got one just before half time, though.'

'How many goals did your side get?'

'None,' she answered angrily. 'They beat us 6-0 if you really want to know.'

'Don't you ever win a match then?'

'Only when we play South Gate.' (This was a girls' school near the town.) 'That's because they've got about three teams, and they send their C team along to play us. Even then it's a struggle. Still, it's all good fun.'

'And what do they call you in the field? Slasher Bennett?'

Someone suggested, 'Tiger Bennett?'

'Or just "The Dumb Blonde"?'

Nurse Bennett went red with anger.

'Oh come on, be sports,' she said. 'I can take a joke, but you go on too much about it. Anyway, I can always get my own back, can't I?'

'What would you do, Tiger?'

'Well, next time you want the bottle, I can keep you waiting for it, can't I?'

'Oh, you wicked old cuss!'

Nurse Bennett walked out of the ward, taking long strides and muttering to herself.

In the evening, Nurse Bennett read prayers in the ward. The only light still lit was a green-shaded lamp on the table where the night-nurse was to sit all through the night. Nurse Bennett read well, and the atmosphere in the ward was suitably devotional, because the patients liked the prayers, and repeated the 'Amens' clearly and reverently. But before Nurse Bennett, walking stealthily on creaking shoes, head bent and hands folded over the prayer-book, had left the room, this atmosphere would immediately be dissipated by an exaggerated belch from Ginger's bed, and a giggle from the postman.

'That's the beans we had for supper, eh, Ginge? They repeat something terrible.'

In a bed in one corner of the room there lay a very old man,

6

who was in hospital owing to a poisoned hand. The postman, who always referred to him as 'that bloody old man', told me about him on my first night in the ward.

'He's a nuisance, because you see he's silly in the head. He thinks he's still at home. He's always taking off his bandages, and he gives the nurses a lot of trouble. He gets out of bed because he thinks he has to get in the coal.'

This was embarrassing, because the hospital was short of pyjama trousers, and few of the patients, among them the old man, wore any. He would choose a moment when there were no nurses in the ward to get out of bed, and would then make for the door which led to the women's ward, and which he believed to be the coal-shed in his own backyard. The old man usually fell down on the floor before reaching the door, and then all the patients would shout 'Nurse! Nurse! Dad's on the move again.' Nurse Bennett would then appear and, smiling cheerfully, and saying, 'Come on, Pop. That's all right, you'll be O.K.,' would lift him up and carry him in her arms back to his bed.

One day there was a new nurse on duty, a young, small girl who seemed struck dumb and almost paralysed by shyness. Nurse Bennett had explained her duties to her kindly and at great length. The new nurse, biting her lip, breathing heavily and staring at the watch which she pulled up from her bosom, clasped my pulse with an iron grip. She took the thermometer from my mouth and brought it into the middle of the room, frowning at it worriedly. Then, her breast heaving, she marked the results of these investigations on my temperature chart with care, terrified that her fountain pen would make a blot. While this was happening, the old man had been slowly climbing out of bed. I called her attention to it. She stared at him, blushing and frightened of his thin hairy legs and shaking movements, and seemed unable to move.

Sister passed the door at that moment, and said to her angrily, 'One of your patients is getting out of bed, nurse. Please will you see to it.'

She approached the old man with diffidence, and could be heard muttering something to him.

Ginger called out 'Pack it in, Pop. You've 'ad it!'

This seemed to frighten the new nurse even more. Fortunately Nurse Bennett came in then, and lifted the old man's legs with her strong arms back into the bed.

From the moment, after prayers had been read and the night staff had arrived, when there was silence and semi-darkness in the ward, until half past five in the following morning when the impatient night-nurse began to take the morning temperatures half an hour before she was supposed to, the old man in the corner talked to himself, loudly and without pausing, whether in his sleep or not it was difficult to determine. His words were impossible to make out; this endless, meaningless conversation continued all night, and made sleep possible only for those patients who had grown accustomed to the noise. The others could sleep for a few minutes now and again, and then the old man's voice mingled with their dreams to disturb them.

I had only one night disturbed in this way. On my second evening in the ward, a doctor, tired of the complaints of the other patients, gave the old man a morphia injection, to keep him quiet for the night. The injection did have this effect; but on the following morning, there was still no sign from the old man's bed, and he lay in this condition, quite still, for three days and nights. The others in the ward missed the diversion which his continual journeys across the room had afforded; they glanced uneasily at his silent bed, and did not mention him. The nurses whispered together. 'It appears he has heart; doctor didn't know.'

On the third day, when we had grown accustomed to the old man's silence, an orderly hid his bed behind three of the green screens which slid along the floor on castors and were always used when it was necessary to isolate a patient for some reason. This was one of the two visitors' days in the week. At two o'clock I could see pass the window a procession of friends and relations, all carrying parcels containing eatables. Some of these penetrated into the ward and clustered round the different beds for two hours. Conversation was at first lively, but at three o'clock it began to flag, and it was usually with a feeling of relief that the visitors rose from their chairs at four, hearing a nurse march up and down the passage ringing a handbell to announce that their time was up. The postman had more visitors than anyone else in the ward, but they came singly and in shifts, and did not stay the full two hours. They were mostly men connected with the post office where he had worked; sometimes his neighbour came with a bag of biscuits, sometimes a sister-in-law with a packet of Woodbines; once a solicitor had arrived, with some papers for the postman to sign, as he had been trying since his accident to get some compensation money, but had so far been unsuccessful.

This afternoon the visitors watched the screens being wheeled round the old man's bed, and everybody knew, without saying anything about it, that he had died under the morphia. The day which had been looked forward to by everyone was therefore spoiled; patients and visitors were depressed by the knowledge that the nurses were washing a corpse behind the screens, and many of them were unhappy that the old man whom they had thought such a bore was dead, as they would miss him. Later on, a woman dressed in green arrived, and disappeared behind the screens. These were then stretched end to end, from the corner to the doorway, and we could hear a stretcher being wheeled behind them. Then they were folded up, and leant against the wall, revealing an empty bed, newly made, the sheet turned down ready for the next patient. The woman in green, who might have been the old man's sister, wife or landlady, sat down in a chair by the fire. She was crying. Nurse Bennett brought her a cup of tea.

'Now, dear, you must drink this.'

The woman shook her head.

'No, you must, it will give you strength.'

Nurse Bennett's voice comforted the woman, and she began to sip the tea.

'I'm going to fetch Sister to speak to you now. You stay there, dear.'

But when the nurse had gone, the woman laid the teacup carefully down on the floor, rose and left the room. Sister came in and, finding her gone, sent a nurse to fetch her. She could not be found in the hospital. She must have walked blindly through the confusing passages, by instinct finding the entrance, and then hurried home through the town to her house in one of its suburbs.

These events were the only things that disturbed the monotony of the hospital routine during the week I spent there. The time was passed staring at the white walls, waiting for the next meal to be wheeled in by Elsie. I was to be taken by ambulance to a Convalescent Home five miles away. My life in the hospital had been lived in a void; in fact, I had hardly lived a life of my own at all, and felt as though I consisted only of eyes and ears to record the few things that happened around me. I had been carried as it were blindfold into the ward, and would be carried in the same condition out of it; I did not know my way about the hospital, or even what it looked like from outside; and if I had been put down at the entrance, and walked out into the town which I hardly knew, I should not have known where to go, and would have lost my way. For a week I had just been part of this white room, like a chair or table in it.

On my last morning there, when I felt as though I had already left the place, an orderly was told to give me a blanket bath, so that I should arrive clean enough to make a good impression on the Convalescent Home. Usually, the blanket baths were done by nurses, and then they were very slapdash affairs. Blankets were modestly heaped on one's shivering body, and only one's arms and legs were washed in tepid water by reluctant feminine hands. The orderly, however, did it thoroughly, and washed every part of me vigorously and conscientiously, even taking the water away to be changed half-way through. He wore a linen mask over his mouth and nose. He had a bad cold, and sniffed and breathed with difficulty behind the mask. When he had finished, he wheeled away the screen, but left the curtain by my bed still drawn. I had only now to wait for the ambulance, and I longed for it to arrive.

As on my first day there, the postman's hand began to draw the curtain back. I would have liked to have spent my last hours in the ward with the curtain drawn, so that I could almost imagine myself alone, and I felt irritated and did not help him to draw it. When he had done so, I waited for the usual explanation.

'I hate to have that thing drawn. It cuts me off from what's going on.' Then he added, 'They used to draw it when my boy lay in that bed by you, so that I shouldn't see him. My hands were bad then so I couldn't pull it back. I reckon it was silly of them to do that, because even if I couldn't see him, I could still hear him call out, couldn't I?'

Matchlight

THE smoke of Woodbines floated up from the plush one and ninepennies to evaporate in the baroque ceiling of the cinema, clouding on its way the flickering beam of light which like a tape connected the small square projection window with the large square screen. A draught stretched down the aisle from the foyer. There were coughs and sighs and the sound of Mars Bars being opened in the cinema. An usherette sat on a stool with a torch on her lap and gazed at the film which was ending.

Although the house was packed, the seats on either side of that occupied by Edna were empty. Edna could not help regarding this as a slight on herself; nobody wanted to sit next to her. Her body had been braced defensively during the programme, her eyes never straying from the screen, for she had never before been to the cinema alone, and did not want to be thought common. If someone had sat by her, she would not have felt so conspicuous, nor dreaded the moment when the yellow lights lit up along the golden walls and she had to stand to attention during the anthem, conscious of the hostile stare of the audience.

Edna considered leaving the cinema before this moment arrived, but decided to stay and see the end of the film. A fair actress sang the sad song which had run through the story in a deep, contented voice, her hair like custard and her cheeks, neck and shoulders like white cushions. On the final note her lover took her in his arms; they kissed slowly and carefully while her slim china hands clasped him in simulated ecstasy. The End appeared on the screen, but one could still see the lovers dimly, and Edna wished she could stop them from fading quite away, for her loneliness, dispelled during the film, must return with accumulated force on their final disappearance.

The crowd pushed out of the theatre into the dark and soon

vanished, each particle of it bound for some room in the spreading town, leaving Edna standing alone and hesitant outside the closed cinema. She did not want to go home yet. The stars provided a faint light, illuminating form and outline but leaving feature and detail to the imagination. The only sounds were those of footsteps far away and once the rumble and whistle of a train. Edna began to walk slowly down the street, singing just audibly the song she had heard in the film, so that a man who passed her turned round to watch her in surprise. It seemed to her that in every doorway in the street a silent couple stood still, pressed so near to each other that they might have been one person. She passed a public house which had just closed, and could see through a window a bar empty but for the proprietor who was collecting dirty glasses.

She came to a bridge over the river which crossed the town, and stopped to look down at the water. The river was like a length of dark blue material on a draper's counter, but the starlight gave it a disturbing radiance. For some time Edna stood there alone, her thoughts confused as though just before sleep. The film she had seen, and her idea that each member of the audience but herself was purposeful and happy that night, made her dread returning to her house, where her mother would have gone to bed having left a jug of cocoa in the kitchen for Edna to warm up on the oven. Her mother believed that she had gone to the cinema with another girl from the office where she worked. Beneath her dark blue coat Edna was wearing a grey satin blouse and a brown woollen suit – her best clothes; it seemed a shame that nobody would know this. How could she take them off, alone in her bedroom, with the knowledge that no one had noticed, and remarked on how nice she looked? She felt pleasantly removed from her daytime life, and somehow superior to every part of it.

When she heard a limping footstep approach she felt obscurely that an unformulated wish had been granted, and her hands gripped the railing of the bridge. She forced herself not to turn round. The steps slackened behind her, passed her, and then stopped. She had expected them to stop, but now she felt frightened. The steps approached her again, and a voice said, 'A penny for your thoughts.' It was almost a whisper, but seemed very loud to Edna.

She turned towards a tall figure, and could just distinguish a long rectangular face, which in the dark seemed to be made of grey leather, beneath a hat with a sharp wide brim. She guessed from the hat, and a note in the voice, that this was an Australian soldier. He carried his shoulders high, and his hands in his overcoat pockets.

'Just day-dreaming,' she said unnaturally. 'Or night-dreaming rather.' She laughed quickly, and turned again to stare at the water.

'Feeling lonesome?'

'Perhaps.'

'Me too.'

'Haven't you friends in the town?' she asked, in the voice she used to address people who came to tea with her mother.

'Christ, no. How should I know anyone in a place like this?'

'You needn't use bad language,' she said, although she had liked the way he said 'Christ'.

'Pardon,' he said, and she was both glad and sorry to discern a note of respect in his voice, which had not been there before.

'On leave?' she asked jerkily, still not turning towards him.

'Forty-eight, and nowhere to sleep.'

'I'm very sorry, I'm sure.'

'You're not very talkative,' he said after a silence.

'I'm not in the habit of talking to strangers.'

'I suppose you want me to push off?'

'No.' Edna faced the stranger, and although her brain was excited her body felt tired and relaxed.

'What I thought was,' he said carefully, 'if you're on your own, and what with me being on my own too, we might spend the evening together.'

'What do you take me for?'

He thought a bit, and then said, 'A bit of all right.'

She thought, 'He can't see me really, that's the blackout,' but she could not help being pleased. She said, 'That's as maybe.'

'Come to think of it, I have got a mate in town. He'd give us a drink.'

'I don't drink.'

'It would be somewhere where we could talk. I like you, and you might get to like me.' He leant towards her so that his coat touched her. 'What about it?'

'I don't mind.' She could hear him breathe deeply, relieved.

'That's it,' he said. 'Hold on half a mo while I light up. Do you want a smoke?'

'I don't smoke either.'

'That's what I like to hear.'

She was happy now. She liked this man – or what she could guess of him, for she could see nothing of him but a lean black shape, with a grey insertion which was his face. The darkness made her feel very near to him, as though already in his arms. They stood isolated on the bridge, above the blue water, with the black forms of houses, factories, churches and gasometers stretching away on either side. She felt all at once confident; her sense of lassitude, shame and fear had passed away.

When he bent his arm to place a cigarette in his mouth she heard a small cracking noise, a sort of squeak; it might have been a shot in the distance but she knew it came from him and wondered what he had in his pocket to cause it. 'Now I shall see his face,' she thought; and then she was blinded for a second by the light of his match. What she did see, in the moment it took for him to hold the flame to his cigarette and suck in the smoke, was a deep purple scar down one side of his thin face. When the match had been tossed over the bridge into the river she remembered also a dark patch over one eye. He had held the match between his thumb and forefinger, and she had seen, but had not registered the fact until it was again dark, that there were no other fingers on his hand – the top of his palm was a flat surface. Now she realised that the squeak she had heard – and heard now once more – was made by the bending of a wooden arm. In an instant she recalled the limp – and the reconstruction was complete. He was not young, perhaps forty years old. He must have been very badly wounded.

'I can't come with you,' she said in a louder voice. 'I'm not that sort of girl.'

She turned round and hurried away. She did not know where she went in the dark; once she bumped against another person walking fast, and once she almost ran into a lamp post. She felt feverish with terror, tears were in her eyes, and she imagined all the time that he was following her, and calling after her. When at last she stopped in a dark side street she could hear nothing but her own loud breathing.

What had he done when she left him? She imagined him still standing there, stunned by her sudden cruelty, deeply hurt, and angry with himself for betraying his deformity too soon. Or had he done so on purpose, to test her and avert a later, even ruder repulsion on her part? She had obeyed an instinct when she ran away, but now she felt the pull of another, contrary one. She could hear his voice in her mind ('That's what I like to hear'); he seemed to be shouting it in her ear while she stood in the street shivering. His voice was kind, and pathetically confident. She felt that she knew all about him; the sort of man he had been before his injuries, and the sort of man he was now. She was embarrassed, and ashamed of her behaviour. She longed to comfort the Australian, to hold his head in her lap and stroke his hair; to prove that she was too fine a girl to be repelled by what he could not help.

She walked slowly back towards the bridge, but was soon lost. Before she panicked, a policeman saw her and asked if he could help.

'Where is the bridge by St Mary's?' she asked urgently.

When he had told her she hurried away, almost running, following his directions. She prayed that the man would be waiting for her where she had left him. She was out of breath when at length she reached the bridge. She walked up and down it, straining her eyes, but there was no one there.

'Where are you?' she asked aloud.

For an hour Edna wandered through the town, gazing into the face of every shadowy figure she passed, walking in circles; but the soldier had disappeared, and eventually, tired at last, she returned to her mother's house, and was grateful for the cocoa in the kitchen.

Davenant Road

I REMEMBER on Sunday morning I slipped out of the house while Mother was upstairs getting ready for church, and hurried down the street. I was myself dressed for church; that is to say, my hat, overcoat, gloves and purse were all dark brown. The street was empty, my shoes sounded loud on the pavement, and I wondered if any of the neighbours were watching me from the dark house windows. I had that feeling you have when you are very excited that someone is behind you, pursuing you; but I did not turn my head until I had reached the corner of the street. There, as I knew he would be, the one-legged man was sitting on the ground next to his sack full of Sunday papers and his cap full of coppers.

I was so nervous and out of breath that for a moment I could not speak; then I said, 'Have you got a copy of the *World Messenger*, please?' This was the name of a popular Sunday paper which we did not take in – Mother only took the *Sunday Graphic*, and would have considered the *World Messenger* common, for it was full of football pools and horoscopes and competitions and scandalous news items. The man fumbled for a long time in his sack, and then he did produce a copy, saying it was the last one. I took two coppers from my purse and gave them to him; then I snatched the paper and went a little way back along the road. I was quite sick with excitement. I had intended not to open the paper until I was back in my room, but I could not wait and unfolded it clumsily standing there in the street. The wind blew it about and I had to hit the pages into position. I remember I was standing outside one of the many private hotels in our street; I could see through a window the edge of a table laid for Sunday lunch, and a table napkin folded in a green napkin ring.

At last I folded the paper at the 'Letters from Readers'

column – and then I suddenly seemed to know for certain that what I was looking for would not be there. Muttering nervously to myself, I looked down the column until I noticed a very short letter printed under the heading 'Colourful!' Was that it? I read the letter through, and only after I had finished it did I fully realise that it was indeed the letter I had posted a week ago. This is what it said:

'Dear Sir,
    I thought it might interest you to know that at the office where I work the boss is called Mr Black, the two typists are called Miss White and Miss Green, and the office boy's name is Brown!
Is this a record or can any of your readers beat it?'

The letter was signed 'Miranda', and in square brackets under the signature was printed, 'Well, readers, can any of you tell of cases which beat Miranda's record? Ed.'

I folded the paper into a tiny square, went indoors and into my room, and put it away under my clothes in the chest of drawers.

At church Mother sang very loudly, but I only moved my lips and did not utter a sound. I never sit through a service without at some part of it suddenly being seized with a desire to scream. It is the thought of the shame and discomfort that would result from my scream that makes me long to more and more. I blush and sweat in my pew during the lessons, afraid that I may lose control at any moment, and shriek aloud, so that everybody in the church would turn and stare at me, shocked and startled. I have never done this, however, although going to church is always a torment for me; I think there must be some little brake in my mind, which works automatically and makes it physically impossible for me to do the disgraceful thing which I perversely long to do.

Anyway, that Sunday I had plenty to occupy my mind, and I sat through the service in a dream. It was the first time I had ever had anything printed in the papers, and for ages that had been my ambition. I had often thought of writing to one of those Advice Columns, but I had no problems about which to consult them, and it struck me as silly to invent one. Once I had written to the Information Bureau of a film magazine asking the date of Jeanette Macdonald's birthday, but the letter was neither printed nor answered. Then I thought of writing about the colour names, which was a good idea as my boss is called 'Mr Black', and I am a typist and my name is 'Miss White', which has always struck me as a strange coincidence. To make better best, I put in that about Green and Brown, which I had invented. I had chosen the *World Messenger* because it was not a paper Mother read, nor were they likely to read it at the office, and it would never have done if someone had noticed my letter, and said, 'Why, this must be from someone at our office!' I would have felt such a silly.

During church I thought of all the millions of people whom I did not know who were no doubt reading what I had written at that moment; and then I thought that of all the copies of the paper printed some must surely survive, and that perhaps in a year's time a man might come across that edition – it might be someone in Africa or China, you never know – and he would read my letter and say to himself, 'Well, that's a coincidence!'

After church as always Mother and I stood about and chatted for a bit in the churchyard with the other people, and then we went home and had lunch together. I believe I behaved quite normally, but all the time I was thinking of the letter in the paper upstairs. When I went to my room after the meal and read it again, I had an odd feeling of disappointment, and felt rather flat. All the week before had been spent in looking forward to that day, and hoping that I would find my letter in the paper; and now that my wish had come true, the letter for some reason seemed very short and rather ridiculous. I remembered that, as a child, after longing for days for some parcel to arrive containing a present, I was not so much disappointed in the gift when it did at last arrive, as sorry that the excitement of waiting for it was over.

I usually spend Sundays with my friend, Mary Conners, who is another typist at the office. We had arranged to meet at three by the bandstand in the public gardens in the centre of the town. I had a little time to myself before that, so I lay on my bed and looked through the *World Messenger*. I came across the following item:

'There has been a further outbreak of anonymous letters in . . . (a London suburb was mentioned). The police say that they are on the track of the writer or writers of these poisonous epistles, and an arrest is expected shortly. The writing of anonymous letters is a particularly despicable and cowardly offence, and any person who may receive one is encouraged to inform the police immediately, and ignore the contents of the letter as they are usually pure fabrications.'

As I had written my letter in such secrecy, I felt a strange sort of connection between myself and the writer of these anonymous letters who depended so much on secrecy for the success of his plans. I imagined him reading that bit about himself in the paper; and surely reading the words 'cowardly' and 'despicable' would give him a thrill, and the whole thing a sense of power? The police, the journalist, and the people to whom he had written – what, I wonder, *had* he written? – were all bewildered by him; he had the power to mystify them, make them wonder about him and fear him. And all by writing a few words on a piece of paper, slipping an envelope through a pillar box when no one was looking . . .

The band was not playing that afternoon, and Mary and I sat on a bench by the empty bandstand without finding anything much to say to each other. It was a dull day, and there were few people walking in the gardens. Suddenly Mary said, 'Oh, look! There's the Black Devil and his family!' Sure enough, there, walking towards us, was our boss, holding the arm of a small stout woman with an uninteresting face, wearing a woolly coat and a pixie hood. They were followed by two little girls with short dark hair. Mr Black himself wore a dark blue over-coat and a bowler hat. He had very black hair and a square face; his jaw, which was cleft, always looked as if it needed a shave – it was a sort of blue colour. That was one of the reasons why we girls at the office had christened him the Black Devil – it fitted in with his name, and also his sarcastic manner, which I think we all disliked. I shall never forget my first day at the office; I was nervous, and all thumbs. I had just got my diploma for typing from Miss Wells in the High Street, but they put me in front of a type of machine to which I was not accustomed. Something happened to the ribbon spool, and the ribbon came billowing out of the machine, making me and everything it touched inky. I could not get it back and it became all knotted and tangled. I was near tears, when who should come out of his office but Mr Black! He took one look at me, and said in that sarcastic voice of his, 'Ah, this damsel seems to be in distress. Can I be of any assistance?' Then he put it right in a few minutes while I stood by, feeling ever such a goose, and now and then trying to help but only getting in the way. Since that day I had never liked Mr Black. He was a man of thirty-odd, and he looked younger than his wife.

To go back to that Sunday in the Gardens. The Black family were still some way away from the bench where we sat when I felt Mary become alert; she was preparing to nod and smile at Mrs Black. I think the acquaintance between them was very slight, but Mary liked to make a lot of it, and many a time had she told me about the day when she went to tea at the Blacks' house, 'Polkerris', in Davenant Road, down near the Station. The houses in that street were semi-detached; they had garages, and short curving drives leading up to the front door – altogether more pleasant than the row of gloomy grey houses in which I lived. I had passed Polkerris several times, and had noticed that the front door, glimpsed between the laurels in the garden, had on it a design of the sun setting behind the sea, suggested by a few steel lines against frosted glass. Mary had told me that the names of the little girls were Hazel and Rosemary. These two children, as they walked behind their parents in the Garden, were playing some secret game with each other, pinching each other's arms, and then stifling their giggles with small fists covered by blue wool gloves.

Whether or not Mr and Mrs Black noticed Mary and myself sitting on the bench I shall never know, but anyway they walked straight past us without so much as a nod, their noses in the air. You would have thought that my boss would have deigned to recognise me outside office hours; and you would have expected Mrs Black to have spared Mary at least a smile after having asked her to tea at her house.

Mary's body relaxed, and she said, 'Well! The stuck-up things!'

I felt sorry for Mary, and I also felt that I had been slighted, as I had been sitting with Mary when she had been cut by Mrs Black. I thought it tactful not to speak for long on the subject, so after a bit I said, 'What about tea at the Regal?'

We did not feel like seeing the programme at the Regal after tea. There were two feature films, but from the advertisements outside the cinema I gathered that they were love stories, of the soppy variety. I do not care for that sort of picture any more, although I used to in my schooldays; and Mary only likes Gene Autry.

I left Mary at her mother's house, and then walked slowly home through the streets which form the outskirts of the town. It was late by now and evening was falling; the dull, dim light hurt my eyes, and made me feel uncomfortable, as though I needed a bath. The dusk seemed to penetrate into my clothes and I felt depressed. The smell that came from a small fish-and-chips shop made me shudder; but when I passed a public house, and saw a door open on a room empty but for a young man leaning up at the bar, I was tempted to go in. Not that I would have drunk a thing; spirits disagree with me; but it would have been nice to sit and listen to the wireless in the bar, which seemed to be broadcasting a better programme than I was ever able to get from our set in the lounge at home. A girl's voice followed me as I walked on down the street: 'How can I resist the Sergeant-Major . . .' I wanted to dance and skip all the way home, but I felt so tired and sad that I could only drag one foot after the other, and stare down at my blue shoes, the laces of which cut into my feet.

As I walked along, I heard a strange voice coming from some distance away, a sound of singing, cracked and mournful. It grew louder as I drew nearer home, and the evening became deeper and the cold more keen. It was a woman's voice, and this is what it sang:

> 'There is a green hill far away
> Without a city wall,
> Where our dear Lord was crucified,
> Who died to save us all.'

My legs took me automatically nearer the house where I lived, but it seemed to me as though I were moving, without my own volition, towards the singer of this hymn. At length I turned a corner and stood looking down a long grey street at the other end of which our house was situated. A Salvation Army lass was standing a little way from me, quite alone, a collecting-box dangling from her arm while she rubbed her naked fingers together. She was singing this same hymn again and again in a cold, tuneless, hopeless voice, the kind of voice in which each member of a congregation in church sings the psalms, believing it to be indistinguishable in the noise made by the others.

There was a sixpenny piece in my overcoat pocket, and I dropped it into her box. She said, 'God bless you!' in between two verses, in a business-like voice; but I felt comforted, and a little of my sadness went away. I walked on down the street, now dark although illuminated faintly by occasional bead-shaded lamps shining through the thin curtains of the ground-floor windows. The woman's voice grew fainter as I went on, but now and then a high note would sound alone and sad above the others, a sort of wail in the deserted streets.

My bedroom at home is very small. Every day it strikes me as smaller than the day before. There are moments when the sound of Mother's breathing and continual swallowing gets on my nerves; when outside it is too cold or dark to sit in the Gardens, and when all the shops are shut and my friends busy; and then there is nowhere for me to be but in my room.

It is important to have something to think about, something secret which not even your family knows. I suppose if I were the type of girl to fall in love, my thoughts would all the time be occupied by some young man; but I am not that sort. No, I like to think a lot about funny little things, so that when I meet a person with a superior smile on his face, I can think, 'Aha! I know something that you don't.' If I did not have these private secrets, I would be very lonely, and my life would be as empty as other people's. As a child I had many secrets; there was Miss Hopkins at school, and during the holidays there was the excitement of waiting for a letter from her. There was that time when I used to take half a crown from Mother's purse every week without her knowing, to buy sweets with; and there were the books I used to get from the Popular Library, books by Michael Arlen and Louis Bromfield, which I kept hidden as no one knew I was a subscriber. Recently this desire to write to the papers had taken hold of me, and I had thought of little else; I re-read my letter in the *World Messenger* that evening, and as I read the printed words I thought to myself, 'I wrote that. I invented those sentences.'

That night, in bed, I could not get the thought of Mr and

Mrs Black and their two little daughters out of my head. When I thought of their rudeness to Mary, I blushed and felt hot, as though I had remembered one of those many bloomers I have made in public – silly things I have said which make people stare at me for a moment, and which afterwards at night I would give anything to take back. When I dozed off, the afternoon's scene in the gardens became muddled in my dreams, and the Black family became confused with words in my head, assuming some other meaning only understood by my slumbering brain, and fighting some obscure combat with one another. All the time I feared Mr Black's blue overcoat, the imagined texture of which mingled in my tired brain with the smooth white sheets to form a continuous humming noise in the room, smooth and sinister in my dream, infuriating me and driving me mad. I could not escape from it; it was a familiar nightmare. My open eyes detected little spots in the darkness, the room I stared at seemed far away, and the night like a dark photograph printed in a cheap newspaper. When I closed my eyes again I saw my boss's Brylcreemed head, the shiny, glossy hair, and the straight white scurfy parting cutting it unequally in two. I heard his scoffing voice, as plain as though he were talking near me, in my room.

At about midnight, I suddenly awoke from these troubled dreams and sat up in bed, excited, my heart beating fast. There must have been an idea hidden away at the back of my mind since the morning; at that moment it came to the surface, as though I had only then thought of it, or imagined it as a possibility. There is no use in writing excuses for what I did that night; the events of the day, as I look back on them now, seem to have been arranged by Fate in such an order as to make my decision almost inevitable. What I thought was this : it would be fun to write someone an anonymous letter of the kind of which I had read in the morning paper. And the person to whom I wished to write was Mrs Black, my boss's wife.

I felt an odd dislike for that woman, as well as for her husband; I did not wish to hurt her, but the idea of disquieting her in such a manner that she could not suspect that I was the cause of her disquiet, appealed to me.

I jumped out of bed and groped my way through the room to the door, where I switched on the light. I put on my dressing-gown and slippers and sat at my little writing-table. On the table was a pad of blue Basildon Bond notepaper, a red stamp-book, and my Onoto fountain-pen with a platinum nib. As I sat there, staring dully at the watermarks on the sheet of paper in front of me, I had a brain wave. If, I reasoned, I wrote to Mrs Black and told her, as I intended to, that there was talk of her husband and another woman, how much I should lessen the chance of my authorship being discovered if I included myself in the accusation! I felt no guilt at the idea of writing an untruth; it was known for a fact at the office that Mr Black neglected his wife, and when I first worked there I used to notice him looking at me in a funny way. So, my tongue wetting my lips in my concentration, and clutching the pen so hard that the bump on my middle finger became covered in ink, I wrote the following, carefully, in block capitals:

'Dear Mrs Black,
    I think you should know that for some time past your husband has been conducting an illicit liaison with Miss Edna White, who works at his office.
                                                    Well Wisher.'

I blotted it carefully, but too soon, so that the blue ink was scarcely discernible against the paper of the same colour; however, I did not feel up to writing a fair copy, so I sealed it in an envelope which I addressed to Mrs Desmond Black at the address which I knew to be hers, taking care to make the letters unlike the ones I usually form when writing in capitals.

After I had stuck on the stamp, I thought that I should never have the courage to send the letter, and was tempted to tear it up; but it seemed a shame to waste a stamp, and I knew that I could never bear to get back into bed knowing that the letter was unposted. I saw now that, while writing the letter, I had never really intended to send it; I had composed it with the care which one uses when playing a game, or drawing for one's own amusement; but now I felt a feverish haste and I began to dress, pulling on my satin blouse and my pleated brown skirt without thinking of what I was doing.

I stood outside in the street, shivering, the little white square which was the envelope shaking in my hand. You will understand what a state I was in when I say that, only after I had walked a few paces towards the centre of the town, did I realise that I was still wearing my bedroom slippers . . .

I was going to post my letter at the GPO because I was smart enough to realise that if I posted it in the pillar box at the end of the street, it might eventually be traced to our district. The moon shone on the houses but did not mitigate their blackness, only lighting the streets and transforming them into gleaming canals, along which my slippers made a slip slop noise which I felt must be audible in every bedroom beneath whose windows I passed. I saw no one, though at one moment, passing a dark telephone booth, I had a feeling that there was a man inside it, watching me through the glass, and I hastened my pace.

Soon I found myself in the High Street, which in the moonlight looked quite different from how I remembered it. It seemed much smaller than usual, like a toy street in a toy town. I noticed that the shops, whose windows seemed so large and inviting when open in the daytime, were merely the ground-floors of ordinary, small, and sometimes quite ramshackle houses. Devoid of people, the town was like a swimming pool drained of water; I walked along the middle of the broad street with the sensation of walking along a dry sea bed.

There were no blinds drawn across the big Post Office windows, and the moon's reflection shimmered in the glass. Oddly enough, the office where I worked was in the same building, on the floor above. Standing there in my bedroom slippers and with some curlers still in my hair, I really believed I was in a dream; so when I posted the letter, and heard it slide on to the base of the box, I merely felt a calm relief, and no guilt or apprehension. I was relieved that my indecision (which had been troubling me beneath the surface of my bewildered mind) could now no longer bother me; I had committed myself once and for all.

I walked home quickly, meeting no one, not even a policeman on his beat. Every day for weeks past, after five, I had made that journey from the office to my home; but that night, owing to the stillness in which I imagined I could discern the deep concerted breathing of all the sleepers in the town, and the absence of buses on the roads and people on the pavements, the distance seemed twice as long as it had ever done before. I entered the house without disturbing Mother and Gladys, and as soon as I was back again in bed, I fell asleep, and this time did not dream.

The week that followed was the most exciting in my life. Every morning I walked to the office with my heart in my mouth, as they say; but when I was there, I was surprised at how easy it was to appear as if I had nothing on my mind. I knew that Mrs Black was bound to receive the letter by the second post on Monday, and that night in bed I visualised the scene of its arrival at Polkerris. I saw Mr Black walk into the drawing-room, tired and cross after his day's work; and I could just picture his wife's face as she sat there, my letter on her lap, and looked up at him seriously. 'I want to speak to you, Desmond. Hazel and Rosemary, run outside and play for a bit, will you? Your father and I want to be alone.' I imagined the following conversation, certain to end in tears; the man shrugging his shoulders and trying to appear at his ease, the woman repeating again and again in a trembling voice, 'There's no smoke without fire, you know.'

On Tuesday I watched Mr Black closely, taking care to hide my interest lest it should betray me, and I noticed that he avoided me. I did not have to look far for the reason for this. Indeed, he scarcely spoke to me all through that long week. I kept a watch on the local paper, but found no mention of an anonymous letter; no doubt Mrs Black had not taken it to the police, and that implied that to some extent the letter had convinced her. I held my breath in horror when I speculated on what complications might result from my action. For some reason, I never considered writing another letter; I was content with the one, waiting impatiently for some indication of its effect, and covertly watching my boss for signs of his unease.

The one occasion on which Mr Black and I exchanged words that week was on the Thursday morning. He came out of his office, and straight up to where I was sitting.

'Oh, Miss White,' he said, looking over my head as was his custom, and with his hands in his pockets, 'I want you to take down a short letter for me.'

'Certainly,' I said, and though I was excited, I noticed with relief that my voice was calm.

He said he wished the letter to have his private address at the head of the page, as it was in fact a private letter. He asked me if I knew what the address was. I thought that this might be a trap of some sort, so I answered 'No'. Then I remembered that Mary, who was sitting a few feet away from me, had once told me where the Blacks lived, after she had been to tea there. I could see that she was listening with interest to our conversation, and although the inconsistency of my reply might never have struck her, I thought it better to be on the safe side, so I added in a nonchalant way, 'I believe I have been told, but I have forgotten.'

So he repeated the address, which I knew by heart, and after dictating a few lines, he took what I had typed for him, and went back into his office. Mary whispered to me 'You've been honoured, dear,' but I did not answer her.

In these days, every night I fell asleep wondering what would happen next, and woke up in the morning with the same thought in my mind. Mother noticed that I was dreamy, and thinking it might be my anaemia that was causing it, gave me a tonic to take. Nothing happened, however, until Saturday. I cannot say exactly for what I had been waiting, but what did occur was not as I had expected.

Mother had gone to the evening service, and as Saturday was Gladys's half-day, I was alone in the house. It was just beginning to grow dark, but I had not yet drawn the blinds, although I knew that when this was done the lounge, which as always by this hour had become untidy and uncomfortable, would at once seem cosier. The sofa and chair covers needed tucking in, and the morning papers lay scattered about the floor; the fire was low. I sat at the window and looked down the street, noticing that the inhabitants of the other houses had also not yet drawn their curtains; the street was studded by the pale lights of indoor lamps. I was tired and thinking about nothing. At that moment I was happy; I was enjoying the inactivity of my life, and if someone had come running up the street with the news that I had been left a fortune, or with a Hollywood contract for me in his hand, I would have been disturbed and annoyed that the peaceful order of my life must be altered. I very seldom felt like this. Usually I walked about in a strung-up mood, expecting something to happen at any moment. This had been particularly the case since I had posted my letter to Mrs Black, but that Saturday evening I was suffering from a reaction, and felt tired and interested in nothing but my lethargic sensations at that present moment. On the table in the middle of the room lay a green ticket; I was going to a whist drive that night in the Town Hall with Mary Conners.

There were few people walking in the street at that hour and so when I saw a figure turn the corner at the far end, near where I had met the Salvation Army lass that memorable Sunday, I watched its progress down the street, paying attention to it with half my mind. This man, who wore a dark blue overcoat and did not have a hat, walked slowly, with his shoulders raised and his hands in his pockets. Only as he passed 'Wychlea', a private hotel five doors from our house, did I recognise the overcoat as Mr Black's. I jumped up from the window seat and took a few paces back into the room, cold with excitement. My peaceful mood was shattered. Of course, he was coming to see me; but I had no time to wonder what this visit might mean, and I stood quite still while his dark head passed the window, waiting for the door-bell to ring. Let him wait, I thought, when at last I heard the faint tinkle in the kitchen; but the second ring did not come and I ran into the hall, afraid that he might go away. Indeed, when I opened the door, he had already turned his back on it, and was descending the four steps to the pavement. If he had been already some way down the street I would have called him back, but as it was I just stood there in the open doorway while the cold of the evening penetrated into the house. He turned round quickly on hearing the door open and looked at me with his eyebrows raised and an embarrassed expression on his face.

'I thought you might be out,' he said.

I did not answer, but looked at him expectantly.

'I hope this isn't a bad time?' he said.

'Not at all,' I answered. 'But do come in, Mr Black. What am I thinking of, letting you stand out there? You must think I'm awfuly ill-mannered. I'm afraid the drawing-room's very untidy. Mother is out. She will be so sorry to have missed you.'

I could think of no more nonsense to say at the moment, and we both stood silent in the lounge.

'Do sit down,' I said, suddenly.

He turned away from me.

'I've got something rather awkward to ask you,' he said.

I thought at once of the anonymous letter, but I could not in that minute realise the full implications of this interview, and I remained quite calm. I said 'Yes?' with just the right indication of a mystified desire to help him, which would have been natural had his words come as a complete surprise to me.

'First, I had better show you this,' he said, and took from his overcoat pocket the letter which I had written to his wife. At first I did not recognise it, so altered did it appear after travelling through the post, and I even for a moment began to hope that I had been mistaken in the reason for his visit, and that it had to do with something quite different. 'My wife received this on Monday afternoon,' he added.

I took the envelope with a puzzled look, which I may have overdone, and I was relieved to notice that the writing on it did appear quite different from my own. I read the letter which had become very dirty and creased since I saw it last. As I did so, I realised with horror that on the table against which my visitor was leaning, there lay my Basildon Bond writing-pad, and also my fountain pen, for I had been meaning to write that evening to my cousin who lives in Hove.

When I had read the letter I could think of nothing to say, and there was a long silence. I was unconscious of my brain working at all, but what I did eventually say showed some subtlety. 'How perfectly horrible, Mr Black. You were quite right to show me this letter. Of course, you have explained to your wife how ridiculous it is – I mean what this horrible letter says?' Even this stumbling sentence, and the clumsy repetition of the word 'horrible' were unnatural and assumed by my brain with automatic cunning to deceive Mr Black.

'Such explanations were quite unnecessary, Miss White,' he said, and I noticed again how absurd it was that our names should complement each other in this way. He had said this with a return to his usual sarcastic manner, and I felt I wanted to slap his silly, big, conceited face.

'I hope you have told the police about it,' I said loudly.

'No, I did not want to do that. The letter is, as you say, ridiculous, and hasn't bothered either my wife or myself.'

Considering the contents of the letter, I thought this remark very rude. I said coldly, 'But the person who wrote it may write others, and may do other people some harm.'

'Yes, we thought about that. It really seemed to have been written by someone who was unbalanced, and didn't mind whom he wrote to or what he wrote, than by someone with a personal grudge, don't you think?'

'Not at all. It might have been written by anyone.'

'I thought I ought to take steps to find out who wrote it, for your sake as well as for mine and my wife's, Miss White. But it seemed to me probable that it came from someone in the office, or someone connected with the office, because there can't be many outsiders who know that you are employed there – and it mentions you by name. So I tried to get to the bottom of the matter off my own bat, as it were.'

'I see.'

The fire was out now, and the room was getting dark; Mr Black and myself stood in it like two shadows with white faces whose features could scarcely be made out. I saw him move his arm, and it seemed to me as if he were taking another letter from his pocket. It was like a nightmare, and for a moment I thought we had gone back a few minutes in time, and were about to play the same scene all over again.

He handed me another piece of paper, saying, 'This is the result of my little bit of detective work.'

I had to turn on the light before I could read what was written on the paper, and I also put on my glasses which were lying by the lamp. I took a long time over this, and Mr Black stared out of the window, drumming his fingers on the table.

'Do you mind not doing that,' I said, and he stopped. From that moment the whole nature of our interview altered. I recognised the paper as that on which I had typed the letter dictated by him on Thursday. I looked up at him as if to say, 'What does this mean?'

'You probably didn't notice just now,' he said, 'that the envelope which contained the anonymous letter had a misspelling of the address. It was the first thing my wife noticed, and we thought it would help us to find the sender. That letter I have just shown you misspells the address at the top of the page in the same way.'

With a terrible feeling of apprehension I looked at the address which I had typed on Thursday, and it seemed to be spelt correctly.

'But I typed this letter,' I said.

'Yes. I meant to test everyone in the office by getting them to spell the address, and I started off with you as you seemed to be the most likely person owing to your name being included in the letter.'

'You dared to suggest . . . you dared to try and trap me . . .' I began in a voice shaking with bitter anger. Then I said, 'But I can swear to you that I never wrote that letter. I don't know how you can imagine such a thing.' He did not answer, and I clutched at his sleeve. 'You must believe me that you have made a terrible mistake.' I noticed with misery that my voice contained the same high, querulous note that it had assumed years ago when I was a child and Mother had discovered that I had stolen money from her handbag. I felt the same as then; willing to swear anything to establish my innocence, and horrified and injured to find that I was not believed.

Still he did not answer, so I said, 'Anyhow, I don't see that it is spelt wrongly.'

'Yes, both times you spelt the word "Davenant" with the "e" and the "a" the wrong way round. You spelt it "Davanent".'

I saw that this was true. I was amazed that I had been unable to spell that word which I must have seen written down several times, while the other word in the address, 'Polkerris', a word with which I was quite unfamiliar and which was much harder to spell than 'Davenant', had apparently been spelt correctly.

'But anyone might have made that mistake,' I said.

'I don't think that is very likely. When I discovered this I did not know what to do, Miss White, but I decided to wait till the end of the week, and then come and ask you privately to discontinue work at the office. We shall, of course, say that it is your wish to resign. I may say that no one knows of this business except for my wife and myself. I have brought with me your salary for another month.'

'I would rather not accept it, thank you,' I said proudly.

'As you please.'

He turned round and began to leave the room. I realised suddenly what he must think of me, now that he knew I had written the letter. I called after him: 'You make me laugh, really you do, Mr Black. I don't know how you can have the conceit to imagine that I should bother to write about you. I really don't. Why ever should I? Tell me that.'

He turned round and smiled at me pityingly.

'That is not my affair,' he said.

I could only look at him then, and I believe I began to cry.

He went out of the house, stumbling against the umbrella stand in the hall. I wanted to run after him and call him back, but I lacked the energy. I saw his head pass the window, but he did not look in at me. I ran to the window and watched him walk quickly away until I could no longer see him for the evening mist.

After that I felt very miserable. I had been so excited about that letter, and now my precious secret which had sustained me through evenings of depresssion was discovered, and I must appear ridiculous in other people's eyes. Besides, what would people say when I ceased to work at the office? Mother would be returning soon from the evening service, and I felt I could not bear to tell her that I had got the sack. What should I think about while waiting for her to come in? I felt that to go up to my bedroom, where the letter had been composed, and where I had spent so many happy hours waiting for the unknown outcome of my posting it, would be intolerable. Outside it was dark and cold. I tore up the whist-drive ticket, feeling that I was destroying a final link with my past sensations.

This despair was unlike anything I had known before. I could not get used to the idea that there was nothing at all that I could do to bring back the past with its feeling of safety and comparative content. The idea came to me to walk out of the house as I was, straight to the railway station, and there to buy a ticket to some distant place, it did not matter where, any village or small town the fare to which coincided with the money in my purse. There I would start a new life, away from Mother, Mary Conners and Mr Black, and all my old embarrassments. But I could not move. I sat in a kind of torpor waiting for Mother to return.

Tomorrow would be Sunday. I remembered how thrilled I had been about my letter to the *World Messenger* a week ago. Then I remembered the Editor's note: 'Well, readers, can any of you tell of cases which beat Miranda's record?' Tomorrow morning, if I bought a copy of the paper, perhaps I would find an answer to my letter.

This thought cheered me up a little.

Punctuality

WHEN I got the sack from the office, I told Mother I had resigned of my own accord, because I could not get on with the other girls.

'Well,' she said, 'and what do you propose to do now?'

'Have a little holiday.'

We were sitting in the lounge near the coal fire. Mother had just got back from the evening service, and she still wore her black overcoat with the fur collar and her black straw hat. Her face was hot and red and shiny under the lamp. She rolled up her knitting and put it on the table by her.

'And who, pray, is to keep you in pocket money?' she asked with assumed politeness, raising her eyebrows.

'I can soon get another job. I can start work again in about a fortnight.'

I picked up the local paper and opened it at the advertisements column. I read out the first one I saw. A young lady of refinement was needed, to sit at the cash desk of the café at the Regal cinema.

'The manageress is quite a friend of mine,' I said. 'I often go there for tea with Mary. I could get that job by raising my little finger.'

'And so,' Mother said in her whining voice, 'I spent all that money on getting you taught to type, so that you should end up behind a counter! And in a cinema, too!'

'I'm sick of typing,' I said, and walked out of the room.

That is how I started work at the Regal. Mrs Taylor, the manageress of the café, said she was pleased to have a girl with a good education at the cash desk, and she added that some of the waitresses were rather common, but I wasn't to take any notice of them. There was only one of them whom I got to be friendly with, Ruby, and she was a very nice refined girl indeed.

I soon got into the way of my new life, and I came to enjoy my work at the café more than I had at the office.

Although the Regal was a big cinema, the café itself was small. There were three entrances : one from the kitchen, a hot poky place from which came a stuffy smell – waitresses were continually getting wedged together in the door; another for the public, at the top of a staircase leading from the foyer; and a third which led on to the balcony inside the auditorium. When this door was opened one could hear for a moment the noises made by the sound-track of the film then playing – an occasional shriek, or the sound of a car or train. One heard always in the café a humming noise, which came from the projection-room just above it : however, one did not notice this as it went on all the time.

The gold walls of the café were decorated with photographs of film stars, all taken some time ago. I sat under a picture of Loretta Young, boxed in by a waist-high wall, with my till and a wireless, which I turned on to amuse the customers whenever I could tune in to a good dance band. The pay was good, and the hours were not long – from four o'clock in the afternoon till ten. From the time we opened until six we had the tea rush; then an hour with practically no custom at all; and from seven onwards people trickled in for supper. We served only pots of tea, bread and butter, assorted cakes, and, for supper, such dishes as beans on toast, welsh rarebit, pilchards, and sometimes a fruit salad as a sweet. Ruby would lean up against the till, and sometimes Mary Conners, the girl I used to be friendly with at the office, would come in for a cup of tea by herself, and when she had finished we would have a chat. I always brought my library book with me (I got a lot of reading done this way), and a writing-pad and fountain-pen in case I felt like writing a letter.

The waitresses all wore green uniforms, but Mrs Taylor allowed me to wear mufti. We had few regular customers : most of them were, as Ruby put it, 'ships that pass in the night'. However, every evening Mr Tillett, the cinema organist, would come in at eight o'clock for a cup of tea and a welsh rarebit, before his turn at a quarter-past. He was a round, bald-headed little man, and always wore a white tie and tails, which looked very smart to the audience while he was playing, but near-to, in the café, seemed rather shabby. Sometimes we would get to chatting. Afterwards, if there were not many people in the café, I would open the door to the balcony, and stand there, at the very back of the theatre, watching Mr Tillett play the organ.

He was a little black speck in the distance, under a mauve spotlight, rolling about on his seat, and it seemed strange that he was responsible for the booming noise that filled the whole great theatre, and also that he was the same person who had sat near me a few minutes before. The words of the songs he played were projected on to the screen, and I would whisper them to myself in time to the music. I clapped loudly when he turned to bow to the audience and then disappeared spinning into the bowels of the theatre. The rest of the audience settled back more comfortably in their seats, looking forward to the big picture which was to follow, but I turned round and went back to my cash desk.

I began to feel as time went on, I don't know why, that Mr Tillett was playing especially for me. In a life like mine one gets used to a sort of routine, and I came to look forward to the moment when the clock hands pointed to eight o'clock and the organist walked into the café, on the stroke, for his evening refreshment.

It was fun to watch the strangers who came to the café, and wonder about them, and try to imagine what their lives were like. One afternoon (it was raining outside, I remember, and the first house had just finished) Ruby passed near me carrying a tea-tray, and whispered as she went by : 'My dear, look at Adolphe Menjou sitting at Number Eight!' Number Eight was a table at the other end of the room, in a corner. A man was sitting there by himself, having his tea. He was not really like Adolphe Menjou, but he had a distinguished, foreign air about him. His hair was dark but streaked with grey, very smooth and plastered near to his head with brilliantine. He wore a blue pin-stripe suit, and I liked the way his tie was knotted. He had more 'class' than any of the other people in the room. His face was thin and pale, and he had large sad eyes, which, from where I sat, seemed to be two black smudges in his face. I could see that he wore a ring on one finger.

I fell to thinking about him, and this made me absent-minded, so that one or two of the girls became quite short with me when I gave them the wrong change, and Ruby said : 'In a brown study?' I thought he must be a stranger in town, and no doubt was changing trains. I got it fixed in my head that he was a bachelor. Perhaps he came from the North.

Then my cash register got stuck. It had never happened before. I fiddled with it for a bit, and then, as ill-luck would have it, Mrs Taylor chose that moment to walk through the café. 'What's up, Edna?' she said.

'I think it's bust, Mrs Taylor.'

But it turned out that there was not much wrong with it, and Mrs Taylor soon put it right. Then she waddled off – she was a fat woman, and wore spectacles. By the time I remembered about the man in the corner of the room, and looked to see what he was doing, he had gone away.

During the lull between six and seven, Ruby came up to me carrying a book. 'Look what somebody's left at Number Eight,' she said. 'I expect it belongs to Adolphe Menjou.'

I looked at it. It was an old copy of *A Tale of Two Cities*, nicely bound. This was one of my favourite books.

'What had I better do with it?' I said.

'Keep it here in case he comes back and claims it.'

I opened the book and looked at the fly-leaf. Written neatly in ink was the following name and address:

> Martin E. Hollingsworth,
> 10 Devon Crescent,
> N7

Meanwhile Ruby went on: 'My dear, he left a bob under the saucer – a change after the usual three-halfpence! I expect it was because he didn't have anything smaller, though, and didn't like to ask. Now, what have I done with Number Seven's receipts? Oh, drat! I must have left it in the kitchen. Dear, dear, my head will never save my heels.' She wandered off to the kitchen. I put the book in my handbag.

That evening I went to bed as soon as I got home, and looked through *A Tale of Two Cities*. I remembered how much I had enjoyed it when I had read it at school. I spent a long time looking at the signature in the beginning, and tried to imagine the man I had seen at the Regal writing it. I thought he had probably bought the book when still at school, and wondered what he had looked like then.

I decided to return the book to him; so, in the morning, I made a neat parcel of it, and enclosed the following note:

'Dear Mr Hollingsworth,

I found this book yesterday at the Regal café, and am forwarding it to you at the address written inside it in the hope that it will reach you safely. I know how sad it is to lose a book one is fond of.

It is strange I should be the finder, as *A Tale of Two Cities* happens to be an old favourite. Of all Dickens's works, it seems to me this is the best.

Hoping you recover it in good condition, I am,

Yours sincerely,

Edna White (Miss)'

A few days later I was surprised to receive a very civil reply. Coming down to breakfast, I noticed an envelope on my plate. Mother, who had obviously inspected it, said: 'Who's your friend?' I did not deign to reply, although I had recognised the neat, well-educated handwriting as Mr Hollingsworth's, and simply slipped it into my cuff. Later I read it in the privacy of my room. This is what it said:

10 Devon Crescent, N7

'Dear Miss White,

Very many thanks for your thoughtfulness in returning the errant *Tale*. I really do appreciate it. After grabbing a hasty cup of tea at the Regal while changing trains on my way to Town after a short holiday on the South Coast, I only noticed its absence when back in the railway-carriage – and have been cursing my carelessness ever since. The receipt of your parcel this morning, therefore, came as a delightful surprise and relief.

I am interested to hear you share my preference for the *Tale*. No doubt we have other tastes in common as well.

Again, very many thanks, from

Yours very sincerely,

Martin E. Hollingsworth'

I read this letter many times. The first time it seemed to me merely a formal acknowledgement of my letter to him, but on re-reading it I thought I saw more in it. The sentence, 'No doubt we have other tastes in common as well,' struck me as particularly significant, and seemed to hint that a reply was expected. At length I decided that Mr Hollingsworth would like me to continue the correspondence. Perhaps my letter had intrigued him: no doubt he would be pleased to receive another one from an unknown girl, whose face and figure he could imagine as he chose. There would be something romantic in a 'blind' correspondence between us, for he did not know that I had any more idea of his appearance than he had of mine.

I had not many friends, and my life with Mother was very lonely. I had often thought of answering one of those advertisements headed 'Lonely', which introduced one to a Pen Pal who shares one's tastes and hobbies. I had also at one time nearly joined a Ronald Colman Club which I had read about in *Picturegoer*: this would have involved a correspondence with another girl who was also mad about Colman, but then I went off film actors; and I hesitated to start writing to a fellow I had never seen – you never could tell, my Pen Pal might have turned out to be a most awful sight! As I had liked the look of Mr Hollingsworth that day at the Regal – something about him had appealed to my imagination, I felt he had a story attached to his past – and as I had the advantage of being to him a mysterious figure, I decided to write him another letter, in the hope of another answer.

I made many fair copies before finally sending one off, and in due course I received a reply. In this way Martin Hollingsworth and I started a friendship which lasted for some weeks. I came to live for his letters, to read them over and over, and kept them stored neatly, in chronological order, in a locked drawer. It was exciting, too, to compose my own: just as exciting as writing a novel or story, even though they were only for the eyes of one person. The days passed without their petty events making any impression on me; I lived in a dream, in a world apart; nothing Mother said could touch me; I sat at my cash desk at the Regal and looked at the other people in the room, thinking all the time: 'Ah! how little you know about me! How surprised you would be if you knew my secret!'

I shall give now the whole of the correspondence which followed on the two preliminary notes. Imagine me in the café, writing and reading the following letters, and hardly noticing the surrounding noise of dishes clattering in the kitchen; women talking over their tea about the shops and their children; the hum from the projection room above; and the disjointed sounds of the films playing, over and over again, in the theatre.

'Dear Mr Hollingsworth,

You may be surprised to hear from me again. But in your letter (received this morning) you say that you wonder whether we both have the same tastes. I have always been a serious girl, and am very fond of reading. Once or twice I have tried my hand at writing, but so far without success, although once I sent a poem to a magazine, and although it was not accepted, the editor wrote me a very encouraging letter.

Skating and hockey are my favourite sports, but I do not get much of them now. If you have similar interests, no doubt you will let me know, and we might correspond? Because there are not many, as they say, "congenial spirits" in this neighbourhood.

Yours sincerely,

Edna White'

'Dear Miss White,

I am intrigued – yes, definitely intrigued. I had hoped – hoped almost against hope – that my last letter to you might elicit a response. And when this morning your letter arrived saying so exactly what I had hoped it might say I thought to myself: "I have made a new friend". Thanks entirely to old Charles Dickens!

Tell me more about yourself – for you have not told me much. I feel there is more, much more to know about you. Have you perhaps a snap you could enclose in your next letter?

As to me – well, there is not much to say. I am a bachelor; I work in the City; I live with my married sister who runs a guest house. I, too, suffer from a lack of congenial spirits around me. Reading is a vice of mine, though I have never essayed to wield a pen myself. Do you belong to the Book of the Month Club?

I prefer golf to either of the sports you mention, and in my younger days was considered quite a dab at squash-rackets. I do not much care for the films, but am a regular theatre-goer. Do you perhaps collect autographs?

Write to me again and tell me more.

Yours very sincerely,

Martin E. Hollingsworth'

'Dear Mr Hollingsworth,

Thank you for your letter. I have not a photo I can lay my hands on, but I can tell you that I am 25, and of medium height. My eyes are brown, and so is my hair – when I was 17 I could sit on it, but now it is bobbed.

I know a bit about handwriting, and can tell some things about you from yours which you have not told me yourself. You are very meticulous, almost finicky, generous to a fault, musical, artistic, proud, a bit touchy. Is that not correct?

I imagine you as tall, dark (perhaps a bit grey). You have large eyes, and a thin sensitive face – a slim figure. How do I know all this? Aha! Call it intuition. By the way, what does the "E" in your name stand for?

I live alone with my mother, my father having died when I was a mite. Mother is a dear, but rather old-fashioned in her views. She will not allow me to have any man friends, and even disapproves of my girl friends – for no reason at all. She does not let me go out much, so I have a dull life. Are you psychic?

Your letters are of great interest to me, and I look forward to them. Write again soon to

Your friend,
Edna White'

'Dear (if I may make so free?) Edna,

Last night I dreamed about you. I was walking somewhere in the country by a canal. It was evening. I came to a lock, and by the lock there was a little cottage with a light in the window. In my dream I knew that you were in the cottage. I waited and waited for you to come out, but nothing happened. Then you appeared at the window for a second – your face was pale and your hair hung long behind your back. You disappeared, and the light in the cottage was extinguished. I awoke with a start.

Write and tell me what my dream meant.

Martin'

My second name is Edgar.'

'Dear Edgar (for I shall call you that),

I do not know the meaning of dreams, although I dream vividly myself. Mother says I live my whole life in a dream – I have always had a faraway look in my eye, as if a creature not quite of this world.

I have an idea. Every evening, at seven o'clock, think of me, because I will think of you and perhaps our thoughts will communicate across space. I have heard of cases of that happening.

Today is the birthday of my little niece, and I am going to tea with her. I love children. They are so gay and innocent.

Write and tell me of your daily doings, because even the littlest things have an interest. And remember to think of me at seven o'clock!

Edna'

'My dear Edna,
Last night, at seven, I concentrated with my eyes closed, and it really seemed for a moment as though you were standing by me. I felt that if I opened my eyes, stretched out my hand, I should see you, touch you. But when I did, of course, all I saw was my little bedroom, empty but for me.

I had considered asking you if we might not arrange a meeting – but no, the time is not yet ripe! Some day perhaps – but for now, let us be contented with this strange spiritual communion, for you are nearer to me than any of my friends, although I have never seen your face. I will not write about trivial matters – they suffice as material for ordinary, everyday intercourse. To you I feel I can open my heart.

I was once very unhappy, when young. I loved a girl, and believed she loved me. Then I discovered that she had been false to me. This incident put me against the whole sex, and that is why I have remained single to this day.

Tell me, Edna, have you ever experienced the sweet agony of love?

Edgar'

'My dear Edgar,
You ask me if I have ever been in love. The answer is yes, once. Of course, I do not count various silly schoolgirl crushes on teachers and actors: we all go through that phase! No, I have only been really in love once, and then it ended sadly. I have never breathed a word of it to anyone, but in you I

feel I can confide. When I write to you I feel like a Catholic confessing : there are none of the barriers between us which are usually between human beings. We do away with pride, shame, embarrassment and so on – at last I can speak with safety of my love for Arthur Crawley.

Two years ago, when my Aunt Pearl, who had occupied the top room ever since Father's death, went to live at East-bourne, Mother decided to let it to a stranger, as she missed Auntie's rent. The first person to answer our advert was a woman in her thirties, with brassy hair and a face covered in make-up. Well, Mother didn't fancy her, so she told her she had better try elsewhere. The next person who came along was Mr Crawley. Mother liked the look of him. I remember coming in one evening, and Mother saying : "I've let the top room to such a pleasant-spoken young man. I think he'll make a nice friend for you, dear. He's upstairs now, having a shave." Mother was always hunting about looking for what she called "nice friends" for me, and they were usually pretty stuffy, so that put me against Mr Crawley. When he came down to supper I didn't think much of him. He was about thirty and looked delicate, but he was dressed neatly and I noticed that he had a nice tie-pin and cuff-links. (I always notice that sort of thing.) He had a job in town, something to do with the railway, but all the time he was with us, Mother and I never discovered exactly what it was.

After supper Mother played the piano, and we all three sang choruses – "Love's Old Sweet Song", "The Mountains of Mourne" and that sort of thing. When he had gone to bed, Mother said : "You ought to be more civil to him, Edna." I didn't reply. I could see Mother had taken a fancy to him.

He used to be out all day, and only appeared for supper, except at the weekends and then he usually went away. We would sit in the lounge for an hour in the evening, and then he would go to bed – every night punctually at the same time. His life was arranged in a routine which he never altered. So I never saw him alone. However, each morning I would do his room (Gladys, the maid, refused the extra work). I would make his bed, and indeed, I was often tempted not to make it properly, but just to straighten the counterpane, fluff out the pillow, and fold his pyjamas, because it was never much dis-arranged. His room was very tidy. He had one photograph – I think it must have been of his mother. His few clothes were always folded in the drawers, his extra pair of shoes always had trees in them. One book – from the town library – would be by his bed. (He never read novels, but seemed fond of biographies and travel.) I would wander round the little room touching his possessions, stand at the window and imagine him staring at the views of roofs which it commanded, and sometimes I would lay my head gently on his pillow. Oh, what a silly I was!

I don't know when it was I began to fall in love with him, as they say, for originally I had not been struck by him at all. I think Mother's hints and suggestions at first had a lot to do with it, though she soon dropped these and took it for granted that Arthur and I would not hit it off – I believe she wanted to think that. She always dominated the conversation in the evening.

He looked so seedy, I wanted to nurse him, feed him up, and make him well.

This went on for some months, and then came that terrible Saturday – a day I shall never forget. I had looked forward to it all the week – ever since Mother had told me she would be at the Missionary Sale in the Town Hall all afternoon, because Saturday was Arthur's day off, and I hoped I might have him to myself until teatime.

When Mother had gone, I sat at the window and waited for him to walk down the street. Soon I saw him coming; he passed the window. I heard the front door open. He looked into the lounge.

"Oh, hullo Edna. Your mother out?"

"Yes," I smiled at him.

"I'm just going to my room for a nap. I don't feel at all the thing. I'll be down for tea."

He certainly did look poorly. I was very disappointed. I would not have my little chat with him after all. I had nothing to do with myself all afternoon, for I had told my girl friend, Mary, that I could not go with her to the pictures that day.

I wandered out into the street, for I felt that I could not stay in the house, or I would be sure to go up to the top room and do something silly. It was a lovely day. I felt lonely. I found myself at the station – perhaps I had gone there unknowing because I vaguely connected it with Arthur. It was as though I were out of my mind. The next thing I knew, I had taken a return ticket to Paddington and was sitting in a train. I thought the other people in the carriage looked at me oddly. I tried to get out again on to the platform, but at that moment the train started. It was a fast one, so now I should have to go to London. I thought even of pulling the communication cord, but then I sat back in my seat and tried to relax. I did feel a fool. Thank goodness, I didn't meet anyone I knew.

At Paddington I walked out through the white Bayswater streets, and into the park. I sat beside the water, and watched children and soldiers feed the birds.

Then I felt that I had to hear Arthur's voice or else I should go mad. I went to a telephone booth and put through a call home – for, as Mother and Gladys were out, he would probably answer. Luckily, I had the right amount of change to put in the box. I could hear the telephone ring in the hall at home. Then suddenly the ringing stopped; a loud voice said "Hello": it was Mother, and she sounded in a bad temper; I hung up, shivering. She must have come home early, I thought. I returned to the station, and waited an hour for the next train back. I bought a copy of *Woman's Journal*, but could not read it.

When I got home, Mother was too fussed to ask where I had been, or to mention the telephone call which must have seemed funny to her. She had come back from the sale early, and had found Arthur ill in bed. The following day he developed pneumonia. For a fortnight she nursed him night and day (she would not let him be taken to hospital). Then he died. Mother cried for days. I think she must have loved him, too.

Only one person turned up for the funeral, a young man who had been at school with Arthur, Mr Robertson; Arthur had been an orphan. Mother and I were the only other mourners. It was pathetic, and I felt silly at the funeral.

Later, without telling Mother, who would have been shocked, I went to consult a medium of whom Mary had told me, who lived in the outskirts of the town. The messages she gave me did not sound like Arthur at all, and I did not know what to think. But soon I stopped minding. I even grew to tolerate Mother's continual weeping and talking about him.

She was always making such remarks as : "I wish you had been more civil to the dear boy, Edna. He must have thought you very stand-offish."

Of course, during his illness, I had never been allowed near his room. Mother took it all on herself. Doctor and Mr Robertson said she had done a wonderful job.

Soon Mother stopped mourning Arthur, and now I only look back on him with a feeling of depression. But sometimes, on a hot Saturday afternoon, I am filled with a feeling – not of love for him, but of a vague longing for something which he had seemed to symbolise.

What a long letter! I wonder if you will read it all. Forgive me if it has bored you.

Edna'

'My dear –

Business takes me near your home again on Friday next. Where and when can we meet?

Edgar'

Picture postcard :

Meet me at 7.30 pm outside the Post Office in the High Street. Don't be late, as I have not much time.

E.W.

I arranged with Mrs Taylor to be free from seven onwards on Friday evening; she herself was going to take my place. I was very thrilled, but nervous too. I do not know which I feared most : that Edgar would turn out a disappointment to me, or that I would be one to him. We had both rather let ourselves go in our letters : would we be able to take up from where we left off, when confronted with each other in person?

Time on Friday moved very slowly. Everything seemed to be as if in a slow motion film; people appeared to take ages paying their bills, sipping their tea; even commonplace remarks about the weather fell heavily from Ruby's sluggish lips, and I longed to say to her : 'Get a move on, do!' Everyone I met had an air of being half-asleep : only I was alert, excited and apprehensive.

At last, at a quarter to seven, I could bear it no longer, and I slipped out of the empty café. I hastened to the Post Office, and as I reached it the clock was striking seven. I still had half an hour to wait! It was raining and evening was starting, so that the street seemed misted, muffled and dim. I knew that I did not look my best in my mackintosh with its pixie cape; my face was shiny and the cold rain made my nose red. I had put on my best shoes in the morning, but now they were hidden by galoshes. How I wished I had chosen an indoor meeting-place!

I thought I should never live through the next half-hour. All sorts of dreary thoughts came into my mind. Suppose he never turned up? Suppose he had been playing a joke on me all along, and intended to blackmail me? Suppose he had been killed in a railway accident on the way? Soon it seemed impossible that the situation could be as I had imagined: had I perhaps dreamed the whole thing? And if, by great luck, he should arrive, what on earth would we talk about all evening? *And what would he think of me?*

This dreadful waiting was familiar to me because I am always early for appointments, even if it is only to meet Mary in the Gardens. I could not contemplate the idea that Edgar might be late: how could I bear to wait a second after half past seven? I regretted my impatience, and wished that I had stayed at the Regal until it had struck the half-hour, so that Edgar would have to wait for me.

There were several other people waiting nervously under the Post Office clock, and I guessed that they were also early for appointments. I noticed a girl of about my own age who was walking up and down, and continually looking at the time, and along the street. There was also a little man who resembled a clerk, wearing a mackintosh, with red hair and moustache and rabbity teeth. He had an evening paper, which he rolled up tight and offered to me: I thanked him and pretended to read it, but I could not concentrate. I stared for ages at an advertisement for lime juice, reading it again and again, but taking none of it in.

I did not know whether Edgar would come from the left or right, but as the station was on my left I faced that direction. At twenty five past seven I saw, with a feeling of relief and excitement, a tall, dark figure coming towards me through the rain, but as he approached, I realised that he was not Edgar, and yet still I hoped, why I do not know, that he would come up to me and, somehow, mysteriously, turn out to be my friend: I was afraid

46

of admitting my full disappointment to myself. Then the other girl who was waiting ran to meet him; they kissed, and walked off arm-in-arm towards an ABC.

To prevent myself from thinking I looked up at the clock, and as I looked away I saw that the red-haired man, who was now standing alone with me, was looking into my face. We stared at each other for a moment, until he suddenly took off his hat (it was a dirty grey trilby) and said: 'Miss White?'

I answered yes automatically.

He held out his hand, after nervously pulling off a glove, and began to stutter: 'I am mmmMartin Hollingsworth . . .'

I realised the truth before he had finished the word Martin. I had taken it for granted that the copy of *A Tale of Two Cities* had belonged to the tall man whom I had noticed: now I saw that it must have been the property of this little clerk, who had sat at the same table earlier that evening, and whom I had not seen and could not remember, for he was indeed very insignificant. Many like him come into the café every day.

I kept my head. 'No,' I said. 'I am not Miss White – I thought you said Miss Wright. You must have made a mistake.' And I hurried away, while he was still stuttering an apology.

I felt sick with horror. This was the man to whom I had written those confidential letters! I hated him, and despised myself. I began to cry as I walked through the drizzle, by instinct returning to the café.

It was empty, and the yellow light hurt my eyes. I hung up my mackintosh and sat at the desk. I heard an actress in the film that was playing in the theatre call out shrilly: 'Help! Help!' That bit always came at a quarter to eight. I was grateful for my solitude. The wireless, turned down low, was muttering at my elbow, and I switched it off. I could hear the waitresses talking in the kitchen.

'Go on!'

'She did!'

'She never!'

'I tell you, she did!'

'Well, I never did!'

I was trying to stop myself from thinking of my recent experiences, but I could not help whispering again and again to myself, 'How could I have made such a daft mistake?' as though confiding in somebody. At length I leant on my desk, with my head in my hands, and wept loudly, out of bitter shame and disappointment.

I do not know for how long I cried; however, I was brought back to earth by a voice saying near me: 'Is anything the matter?' It was Mr Tillett, who had come into the café without my seeing him.

'It is a personal matter,' I said.

'Is there anything I can do?'

I blew my nose in the hankie which I keep under my desk, and smiled at him. 'I'm all right now,' I said. 'Please don't speak about it any more. I'm very ashamed of myself for giving way.'

'I was going to ask you, Miss White,' said Mr Tillett, 'if you would do me the honour of lunching with me one day next week?'

I was surprised to hear this. We arranged to meet on the following Monday at the Kardomah. He patted my shoulder, and left the room.

Then I felt better. It is funny how things cheer you up. Mr Tillett was no oil painting, but he was a gentlemanly sort of man. I decided to write to Martin Hollingsworth (the real Martin Hollingsworth, the seedy little clerk I had just left, not my Edgar, the man I had glimpsed for a moment weeks ago, whom I would never see again, who did not know that I existed), and say that I had been unable to keep the appointment owing to illness, and was leaving the town. I would say that Mother had found one of his letters, and that he must write no more, as she threatened to have the law on to him. He would never know that he had seen me at the Post Office.

I felt quite calm now. To fit my mood, as it were, the café was suddenly filled with the sound of beautiful organ music – Mr Tillett playing 'Ah! Sweet Mystery of Life!'

Temptation

O N this hot Saturday afternoon, girls in cotton dresses and men in bright blue suits wandered arm-in-arm through the streets towards the swimming-baths, and children stopped every so often on the pavements to lick their ice-cream cones. A brass band played in the Public Gardens and the shops unfurled their awnings. The clock-face on the Town Hall glittered; the High Street was busy and the suburbs were still, for the people of the town had dutifully left their houses, forgoing their afternoon rests, to take their pleasure in the heavy, sticky air.

Edna, at a loss, ambled through the streets, walking like a child only on the squares of the pavements and trailing one hand along the railings which she passed. From her other hand dangled a shopping-bag containing her purse, a cauliflower and a tin of Vim. It was her afternoon off.

She stopped at a small bookshop, and looked in at the window where she saw spread out copies of bright-covered magazines : *Psychology, Health and Strength, Graceful Poses, Film Frolics.* 'I wonder if they've got a *Picturegoer,*' she said to herself out loud, and turned through the door of the shop.

It was a box-like room of which three walls were lined from top to bottom with books, while the other consisted of the door and window. By the window stood a chair and table; on the table a till had been placed, and on the chair a fat, swarthy man was sitting, reading the *Daily Mirror.* He had hung his coat over the back of the chair and rolled up the sleeves of his collarless shirt. His yellow braces wrinkled over his fleshy chest and the top button of his trousers was open. Edna did not like the look of him at all.

She asked him if he had a copy of the magazine she wanted. Without looking up from his paper, the proprietor said 'Sorry,' and slightly shook his head.

Well! thought Edna. She decided to look round the shop. The sun shining through the window heightened the different colours of the books on the walls. The man paid no more attention to her.

She wandered round the room, now and then reaching or stooping for a volume which caught her fancy, reading a line or two, and then replacing it on the shelf. When she came upon an expurgated copy of *Lady Chatterley's Lover*, she automatically stretched out her hand towards it, but then stopped herself and stood still. What had she heard about this book, and why did its title intrigue her? She was aware of some mystery connected with it, some reason for hesitating before she inspected it. Then she remembered an incident in her childhood.

She must have been twelve or thirteen at the time. Her mother was entertaining a friend at tea. Edna recalled this friend's shocked voice: 'There she was, sitting up in bed, reading *Lady Chatterley's Lover*! "Wherever did you get that, young lady?" I said. "Jim gave it to me," she said. "You hand it over to me this minute, and be quick about it," I said. Disgraceful! They oughtn't to print such things, to find their way into the hands of young girls.'

Edna's mother said, 'What a thing! I wouldn't have it in the house.'

They had forgotten Edna, who interrupted: 'What is it about, then?'

The women looked alarmed. 'Never mind,' her mother replied. 'It's nothing that would concern you.' And the friend added, 'Little pitchers have big ears.'

Standing in the shop, Edna also remembered that shortly after that conversation she had overheard two girls at school giggling over the same book. She often wondered about it then, and afterwards the name lodged itself in the back of her mind, still surrounded by an atmosphere of wickedness and fascination.

Now was her chance to explain and dispel that atmosphere. She must buy the book. It would be simple to conceal it from her mother, who no doubt would still disapprove of Edna reading it. However, she felt embarrassed at the thought of buying such a book from the unpleasant man sitting behind her.

She had been for some time trying to gather enough courage to pick out the novel and ask the proprietor its price, when she suddenly realised that her purse contained only a few pennies. She moved away, took another book in her hands and pretended to look at it, while her mind dealt with the problem. If she returned to the house for more money, her mother might waylay her; soon it would be closing-time, the shop would shut on Sunday, and she would be working all of the following week and unable to buy the book. By next Saturday it might be sold to someone else. The easiest thing to do was to steal it.

From then on she acted with instinctive cunning. Replacing the other book, whose title she had not noticed, with a gesture to imply, in case the man was watching her, that after all she had decided against it, she returned to her former position. She looked over her shoulder; the fat man was engrossed by a comic strip in his paper. Very quickly, she reached for the book she wanted and slipped it into her shopping-bag between the Vim and the cauliflower. The shape of the bag was not much altered. Then she put up her hand, apparently to finger yet another book, and arranged the loosened volumes so that the absence of one should not be noticed. Again she glanced, in the airiest way possible, over her shoulder, but detected no move from the man.

Her instinct was to hurry at once with her booty from the shop, but she checked it. She forced herself to wander once more nonchalantly round the room, staring unseeing at the walls. At last, after what seemed to her an age, she turned at the door to say, 'Good afternoon' to the bookseller. For the first time he looked up at her. Did she imagine suspicion in his small dark eyes? 'Afternoon,' he mumbled, and turned back to the *Daily Mirror*. It struck her for a moment that there was something sinister in his lack of observation; he might have been all the time daring his customer to steal.

She did then hasten away. Walking as fast as she could without running, she moved blindly on through the crowded town. Her imagination, numbed during her theft, began to work again. Did the man have some check on every book in his shop; would he miss the D. H. Lawrence, remember her, set the police on her? Would she go to prison? Had he noticed, through the shop window, while she made her escape, a bulge in her leather shopping-bag which had not been there before? Was he following her at this moment? She hurried on.

She passed the deserted suburbs, the gasworks and the station, her lips moving in a torment of uncertainty, and eventually found herself outside the town. She halted, out of breath, and turned her head. No one was following her; a few people were strolling along the dusty road, come to breathe country air among the fields. Edna climbed over a stile, and took a path to where a stream ran between willows. Here she sat, and in the shade of a tree began to read her book.

She sat on until the air cooled and midges began to worry her bare legs. She finished the book with her eyes aching, and a feeling of acute disappointment. She had not enjoyed it; after skipping impatiently, all the time expecting a passage of a revelatory salaciousness, she now felt dizzy and even cheated. Reading it too quickly, she had not always followed what she read. Nothing was satisfactorily explained.

Church bells were ringing in the town. Edna rose from the grass, and stretched her stiff limbs. She leant over the stream, and, after making sure that no one was near, she dropped the novel into the water. It sank into the muddy bed, and soon could not be seen. Glad to be rid of it, she knew that she need worry no longer, for even if the theft were discovered and suspicion fell on her, how could they prove it now?

Swinging her shopping-bag, her skirt stained by the grass on which she had lain, she walked slowly back through the green and yellow fields to the town.

It's Not Very Nice

'No,' said Mrs Lyddiard, 'I wouldn't be in Hitler's shoes now for all the tea in China.'

'Speaking perfectly frankly,' said Mrs Mitchell, 'I don't trust Stalin an inch. I wish I did, but I don't.'

Mrs Lyddiard sighed. 'Well, we must put our faith in Winston, as we did before.'

'And what do you think about it all, Agatha?' said Mrs Mitchell. 'You're the brainy one of the family.'

The two middle-aged women turned with angry expressions on their broad faces to the girl who was sitting in a dark corner of the room.

'I'm afraid I wasn't listening to your conversation,' said Agatha Lyddiard after a hesitant silence. Her mother and the visitor clicked their tongues, exchanged a look in the darkening drawing-room, and concentrated again on each other.

Outside the high bow window, which had a window-seat running along it between heavy dark green curtains, evening was slowly hiding the grey street with its porches, shrubberies and conservatories. Inside the room Agatha could hardly see the two women, the tall bead-shaded lamps standing here and there unlit like sentinels, the Japanese cabinet or the many small tables supporting bric-à-brac, although all these things were faintly illuminated by an electric fire in the draughty grate. The fire was made to resemble glowing coals, and flickered by artificial means. The tea tray had just been carried from the room.

Agatha was eighteen; she had brown hair which hung untidily, a good-looking face and a dumpy figure. She wore ankle-socks and a wool dress rather like a school tunic. She looked intelligent and resentful, and would have been attractive had she taken more trouble with her appearance. Her mother, a doctor's widow, was a large, bossy, and yet very feminine

53

woman, with neat, greying hair and a white, pretty face. Her friend, Mrs Mitchell, was a less successful variant of the same type.

Agatha listened vaguely to the conversation, which, after touching on Mr Eden and the Princesses, turned from public figures to personal interests, such as the difficulty of getting 'staff', and the lack of a fourth at bridge in the neighbourhood. After a short literary interlude, during which the latest Daphne Du Maurier was discussed, the talk reverted to Agatha, although she herself was not addressed.

'What does Agatha find to do with herself all day?' asked Mrs Mitchell.

'She's waiting to be called up by the WAAFS.'

'Well, that will make a change for her. I do hope she's with a nice type of girl, they say that makes all the difference.'

'She had set her heart on Oxford, but of course in wartime one cannot pick and choose,' said Agatha's mother cheerfully.

'My Evelyn brought her commanding officer to tea with me the other day. A delightful woman. Evelyn has been very fortunate.'

Agatha restrained herself from interrupting the others; from assuring Mrs Mitchell that she did not want to go into the WAAF, and that she easily could have gone up to Oxford if her mother had approved. Such an interruption would only have convinced Mrs Mitchell that what she already suspected was true – Agatha was a 'highbrow'. This was a word which neither Mrs Mitchell nor Mrs Lyddiard used lightly, and, when they did, only in hushed tones, as though afraid that, if they were overheard, they might be involved in an action for slander. At last the conversation degenerated once more into a grumble, and the shortage of food, petrol, and, above all, servants, was examined in all its aspects with a hopelessly indignant, impotent and yet vaguely comforting thoroughness.

'I'm sure Beryl steals my face-powder. If I say anything, she threatens to leave. What can one do?'

'Exactly, what can one do?'

'I suppose I ought to be thankful to have *someone*. All the same, it's not very nice.'

'No, it's not very nice.'

Agatha got up from her seat with an effort. 'I'm going out now,' she said. 'I won't be in to dinner.'

'Might one make so bold as to enquire with whom you are dining?' asked Mrs Lyddiard, and Mrs Mitchell giggled.

'With Mary. Can you see the book I'm reading?'

Mrs Lyddiard picked up a volume and looked at its title with screwed-up eyes, and a patronising smile on her face. 'I suppose this is it, it certainly doesn't belong to me. Can you really understand French, or is it only show?'

Mrs Mitchell laughed politely and said, 'Oh, don't be killing, you know she understands French. After all, she's the latest from school.'

When Agatha left the room the others were talking about their schooldays, and complaining of the rustiness of their French. Agatha suspected that soon Mrs Mitchell would say, 'I thought Agatha was looking rather seedy at tea,' to which Mrs Lyddiard would reply, 'She's at a very difficult age. I shall miss her when she goes into the WAAF, but I expect it will make a new woman of her. It's all wrong she should be kicking her heels at home.'

Agatha put on her coat in the hall and hurried down the porch steps with the book of poems in her hand. At every window in the street she glimpsed a dim interior identical with the one she so gladly left behind. She walked towards the centre of the town, and stopped for a moment at the Repertory Theatre, which was just opening its doors, to look at the photographs of the actors which hung in the foyer. She stood opposite one which showed a thin, handsome face with straight fair hair, perfect for the young hero in almost any play. This was John Taylor, the youngest member of the company; Agatha was going to spend the evening with him, for he was not acting that night, but was to take the leading part in *The Vortex*, which would be playing the following week. Agatha stared at the photograph, and she knew that this anticipatory pleasure was greater than any she would feel in the company of the original. At last she combed her hair, pulled at her dress, and walked with controlled haste to a boarding-house in a street not far away. Had her mother and Mrs Mitchell seen her now, and noticed her guilty air, they would have been in a way satisfied, to find justification in their vague suspicions of Agatha's behaviour when she was supposed to be out with Mary.

Johnnie Taylor lived in a small room on the ground floor of the boarding-house. There was little room in it for anything but the narrow bed and enormous chest of drawers with which it was furnished, and the pattern on the wallpaper haunted his dreams and made them nightmares. Johnnie could have afforded better lodgings on the salary the theatre gave him, but he stayed here because the landlady had taken a fancy to him.

Agatha put her head round the door and said, 'Can I come in, Johnnie?' The room smelled of cigarette smoke, and she knew that the window had been closed all day. Johnnie lay on the bed wearing only a white shirt and grey trousers. In reality his appearance differed subtly from his photograph; he seemed on a smaller scale and his good looks were less conventional. His hair flopped from its parting in a smooth square over his forehead and one eye; he looked delicate. All his friends, including Agatha, pitied him, but with a safe sort of pity to which they could abandon themselves without fear of too great a demand on their emotions, for they knew that beneath Johnnie's apparent fragility there was a hard, tough core of self-sufficiency. Pity for a deserving object is not a pleasant feeling and people steel themselves against it; Johnnie inspired the other kind, and exploited it.

'Oh darling,' he said, a slight North-country accent perceptible in his stage voice which was modelled on Noel Coward's, 'I'd forgotten you were coming. I ought really to learn my part this evening.'

Agatha sat on his bed and smiled at him. 'Do you want me to go?'

'No, stay and cheer me up. Did you like the book?'

'Very much, I want to talk to you about it,' she said eagerly.

'Oh God, darling, *not* an intellectual discussion this evening, if you don't mind. I couldn't face it.'

Agatha dropped the French poems on the bed with such a hurt expression on her face that Johnnie had to turn away. He went on in a softer voice.

'I got a letter from Christopher this morning. It's made me so unhappy.'

He turned round to look at her again, critically, as though examining a picture. Agatha stared at the window with assumed unconcern, but one eyebrow was twitching nervously under his inspection.

'What have you done today?' Johnnie said suddenly.

'Nothing. Mrs Mitchell came to tea.'

'Who's Mrs Mitchell? Tell me about her.'

'Well, she has a dog called Keith Prowse.'

'How extraordinary. Why?'

'He's always sitting on the best chairs, she says, and covering her cushions with black hairs,' Agatha explained in a dull voice. 'You see, it's a joke about the advertisement – You want the best seats, we have them.'

Johnnie laughed loudly. 'Oh Agatha, what wonderful people you know. You are lucky.'

'They're not a bit wonderful really. They sound funny to you when I tell you about them, but you wouldn't think so if you lived with them.'

Johnnie took her hand and pressed it.

'It is nice to be with you, darling,' he said.

Agatha smiled at him happily and for some time they said nothing.

In spite of her wish to appear intelligent and sophisticated, Agatha's voice sounded now and then like a child's.

'Johnnie, if you could have one wish which would come true,' she said at last, with ingenuous eyes and a slightly self-conscious manner, 'what would you wish?'

'To be offered a good part in the West End, I suppose. Anything to get out of Rep.'

'But that's bound to come true soon.'

'No, never, probably. I'm such a bloody actor.'

'Oh, darling, I think you're wonderful, I think –'

'What would you wish?' Johnnie said quickly.

'To go away from here. That is, only if you are leaving.' He patted her hand and smiled absently at this. She went on, 'Oh, I suppose I should wish for mother to send me to Oxford instead of going into the WAAF.'

'God forbid, darling. I should hate you if you were an undergraduate. You're quite serious enough as it is. No, what you need is some terrific man to have a love affair with you. If I was only normal, I'd be just the person. Goodness, sweetie, you're blushing; you're red all the way from here' – he put his finger at the neck of her dress – 'to here' – and he touched her forehead. 'You are very virginal, aren't you?'

'Do you like that?'

'As long as you don't overdo it.'

'And do I overdo it?' Agatha asked very earnestly, leaning towards him. 'Do you think so, Johnnie?'

He jumped off the bed and began to put on his tie, socks, shoes and coat. 'I'm so hungry,' he said, 'let's go to our Milk Bar.'

It was quite dark outside now. They walked, arm in arm and singing softly, towards the Milk Bar where they usually ate. Although it was painted white all over, it was a dingy place, with an angry girl standing behind a wet, sloping counter. They sat on two high, uncomfortable stools and each ordered spaghetti pie and a strawberry shake.

'Do you remember when we first saw each other here?' said Agatha. 'What did you think when you saw me sitting here by myself?'

'I thought, what a beautiful girl, I should so like to make friends with her. What did you think when I spoke to you? Did you think I was making a pass at you?'

'Yes. I was very excited.'

'And were you disappointed when I didn't?'

'Oh *no*! How can you ask that?'

'We have a lovely friendship,' said Johnnie sadly, and, it seemed to Agatha, with no conviction in his voice. 'You're the only person in this place I can stand.'

'And you're *quite* the only person I can talk to,' said Agatha. 'I don't know anybody else who likes the same things as I do. You make all my other friends seem so boring. When I'm with you, I dread going back to the house and hearing Mother's conversation and never being able to talk about books and pictures and things, or laugh like we do sometimes. If it wasn't for you, I'd go mad.'

'What would your Mother and that wonderful Mrs Mitchell say if they could see you now?'

Agatha thought for a bit. 'Mother would probably say, "You know, Agatha, really, it's not very nice, is it?" And Mrs Mitchell would repeat after her, "No, dear, it's not very nice." '

'And neither it is,' said Johnnie glumly.

A couple who had been sitting in silence at the bar now left the room, leaving Agatha and Johnnie alone with the waitress, who pulled a tattered book from behind the tea urn and began to read it, now and then glancing aggressively at her two customers as though she wished they would leave. Johnnie stared at his reflection in a mirror opposite him with a secretive look, giving the false impression of being absorbed in his thoughts. Agatha was not enjoying herself. She dared not talk naturally, for fear of being thought pretentious by Johnnie, and she was trying hard to think of something that might amuse him. The more desperately she searched for a sentence with which to break the terrible silence, the blanker her mind became, until, in a voice made unnatural by over-deliberation, she brought out, 'I went to a funeral yesterday.'

'Did you? Have you been to any more dances at the golf club? Let's go, darling, this place is getting me down. Have you any money on you, sweetie?' Agatha paid, and soon they were standing together outside the bar in the cold street.

'Listen,' said Johnnie. 'Would you think it awfully rude of me if I left you now? I've just remembered I promised to meet Tony at the Castle bar after the show tonight.'

'But, Johnnie, I've hardly been with you at all.'

'I know, but I really ought to meet Tony or he'll be furious, and there's no use in my bringing you too because you'd only be bored stiff.'

Agatha said in a trembling voice which she could not control, 'You hate being with me, don't you? I bore you.'

'Oh, for God's sake don't be difficult. You know I love you, Agatha, but I'm in an awful mood tonight and I can't help it. That letter upset me, and I know I shall be bloody in the play next week. Please understand.'

Agatha steeled herself against his pleading voice. 'You don't like me at all really. You only pretend to. You only see me at all because you want to be seen about with a girl occasionally instead of your awful men friends like Tony and Christopher.'

'Don't shout, do you want that woman in there to hear everything you say? And what a bitchy remark, Agatha,' said Johnnie in a genuinely shocked voice. 'You must be mad. Who is there to "see me about with you" anyway? You're so ashamed of me, you're so afraid your idiotic family will find out about me that we never go anywhere except to this squalid Milk Bar. If that's what you think I'll leave you now.'

He began to walk away, and Agatha called after him in an agonised voice.

He came back, put his hands on her shoulders, and said gently, 'It's all right darling. I know you didn't mean what you said

59

and neither did I. Come round tomorrow evening and I may be in a better mood. I must fly now.' He gave her a long, careful kiss on the mouth and walked off once more, his head bent and his shoulders hunched.

Agatha's body had been tense during the kiss, but she relaxed as she watched him disappear. She nearly called after him, 'Do up your coat, or you'll catch cold,' but stopped herself as she knew this would irritate him, and be marked up against her in his mind for use in a later quarrel. Her evenings with Johnnie often ended like this; he kissed her, spoke to her kindly and affectionately, forgave her tactless outbursts, but still he conceded nothing. He always managed to do as he wished, to elude her completely, and yet make it appear as though she were in the wrong. Now Agatha longed to follow him, and could hardly bring herself to move in the opposite direction; at last she began to walk slowly towards her home. Soon she came to a traffic roundabout in the middle of the town, and sat down on a bench beneath the War Memorial. She wanted to clear her confused brain, to check her steps which would lead her too soon to her mother's drawing-room.

Sitting in the dark, with the noises of the town going on round her, Agatha looked on her life in a detached way. She saw it as though from a great distance, and as if it had nothing to do with her. On one side, as it were, was her home life; here she saw herself bored and misunderstood. In contrast with this was the time she spent with Johnnie; she was never bored with him, but neither was she happy in his company. She loved him, but he defeated and frustrated her. During the day, with her family and the few friends of whom Mrs Lyddiard approved, Agatha seemed to exist only by looking forward to her next secret meeting with Johnnie; with him, she was saved from complete despair by the knowledge that behind her was her home and some form of security.

At moments like this, Agatha thought with a tremor of excitement of the possibility of suicide. Many times had her mind followed the same routine; what if she rose from her seat, and threw herself under the wheels of the car now coming down the High Street? For a second this seemed a frighteningly easy thing to do; then Agatha realised that it was out of the question, that even if her mind decided on the action, her body would not obey it. Next she imagined an attempted suicide, prevented at the last moment by something beyond her control. She saw herself lying in bed, injured, treated by everyone as a heroine; her mother would blame herself for her daughter's desperate behaviour and Johnnie would read of it in the papers and hurry to her side, white with anxiety. There, at last, would be a situation! After thinking of this for some time, Agatha began to feel sleepy and rather hungry, and decided to delay her suicide until the next day, and perhaps even abandon it altogether; she suddenly appreciated two great blessings of life, sleep and food.

At one time Agatha had comforted herself at such moments of depression by imagining unlikely successes for herself. '*Fever*, the brilliant novel from the pen of a new young authoress, Agatha Lyddiard, has been acclaimed by all the critics as the book of the decade. We feel that Proust would have been proud to have written it.' 'Agatha Lyddiard, a new young actress, caused a sensation last night by her interpretation of Hedda Gabler. The greatest artist since Duse . . .' and so on. Now these dreams only depressed her by their futility.

Soon she began to feel that things were not so bad after all; she was seeing Johnnie tomorrow. She walked uphill towards the 'residential district' on the outskirts of the town. As she neared her home, she noticed that the drawing-room lamplight was glimmering feebly through the green curtains. In the hall, she was depressed once more by the smell of furniture polish and the sight of the wide, dark staircase; she was about to climb the latter, when she heard her mother calling from the drawing-room.

Mrs Lyddiard was sitting by the fire with a car rug over her knees and a book open on her lap. She was reading and knitting at the same time. She took off her spectacles and smiled at her daughter.

'Well, dear, did you enjoy yourself? How was Mary?'

'Very well,' said Agatha. She sat down and folded her hands patiently.

'I missed you this evening, darling,' said Mrs Lyddiard. 'I suppose I shall have to get used to dining alone. It will be rather beastly for me when you go away, but I mustn't be selfish. I've been thinking this evening, by myself, what a thin time you have of it here. There are so few people of your own age, and you really ought to know some young men. I expect you'll go to Air Force dances, and perhaps you'll meet a nice type. Agatha,' she said, leaning forward and smiling, 'I want you to feel always that you can bring your friends home here, and be certain of a welcome. Background is so important for an unmarried girl.'

Dear Derek

M<small>RS</small> L<small>YDDIARD</small> had not seen her godson, Philip Hall, since his christening nineteen years ago. She had been able to follow his progress since then with tepid interest, for news of it filled the letters she received now and then from his mother, Lettice Hall, a friend of Mrs Lyddiard's youth whom she now never met. When one of these arrived, containing not only the latest bulletin (Philip had just finished his first year at Oxford), but also the request that the Lyddiards should put him up for the last week of the vac while Mrs Hall dealt with some vague domestic crisis, Mrs Lyddiard's first thought was, 'He might do for Agatha.'

Although Agatha spoke little of Philip before his arrival, she was looking forward to his visit. She had gathered from her mother – and to Agatha his being an Oxford undergraduate implied – that he was an intellectual. She thought of herself as artistic, and expected Philip to be better company than the dull young men who lived in the neighbourhood. She had learnt, however, always to prepare for disappointment, and so as a kind of mental insurance policy she discouraged herself from hoping too much of him, and whenever her mother said, 'He'll be company for you, dear,' she answered, 'I don't know, he may be frightfully boring, or pretentious, or something.'

People are always at a disadvantage arriving at a house, particularly a strange one, and even more so when they do not know that they are observed (although they may suspect this). Agatha had posted herself, on this longed-for morning, at the first-floor landing window, and when she saw Philip turn down the street, carrying two heavy suitcases, she was surprised to see him so young; she had forgotten that boys of nineteen seldom look mature. His face, which was not spotty, but looked as though it recently had been, was pale and broad, with handsome features.

63

His brown hair was tousled. If Agatha felt disappointment at this first sight, it was not keen. His clothes were as she had expected: corduroy trousers, dark shirt, red tie and tweed jacket, and she found that they suited his tall figure.

Conscious of her mother restless in the drawing-room, near the window but not at it, Agatha hurried to her bedroom when the front door bell rang. She could well imagine Mrs Lyddiard's embarrassing welcome of her guest, and meant to give it a miss – ('The last time I saw you you were a toddler; isn't it fantastic? What sort of journey did you have? *How* is your dear mother? We *never* meet now . . . but you must be feeling fearfully grubby, let me show you your room.' Then, over her shoulder as she preceded him upstairs, 'We're a household of females, you know. I hope that doesn't alarm you!') Agatha had decided not to make her entrance until Beryl had beaten the gong for lunch. She knew that Philip had only the vaguest idea of what she would be like, and hoped to surprise him pleasantly, now that she saw from her secret observation of him that it would be worth trying. She felt slightly ridiculous, however, sitting firmly and unnaturally on her bed while she heard him unpacking in the room next to hers. She sat out his session in the bathroom, praying that her mother would not call her, and though the echo of the gong had long faded in the hall, she waited until he was safely back in the drawing-room, before she slowly walked downstairs.

Mrs Lyddiard ponderously replaced her empty green coffee-cup in its saucer. They were sitting in the drawing-room, all three feeling sleepy after an indigestible lunch. She rose heavily from her chair. With an expression of conscious tact, which Agatha hoped was not as obvious to Philip as it was to her, Mrs Lyddiard said, 'I've got to be off now to a Red Cross lecture. I'll be back for tea. So, Agatha, you must entertain Philip till then.'

Agatha looked distant; rather clumsily, Philip raced his hostess to the door, and just succeeded in opening it for her before she reached it. Alone together, the two young people were silent for what seemed to Agatha a long time.

She was pleased at last to see him notice a novel by Aldous Huxley which she had placed on a table that morning.

'I see you're an admirer of Huxley.'

Agatha had realised at lunch that Philip was shy of any enthusiasm, and so she altered the speech which she had prepared for this moment.

'His early ones amused me, but now I think he's getting rather tedious.'

She could not tell what he thought of this, but it seemed to her a foolproof remark.

Philip looked about him, more at his ease since Mrs Lyddiard's departure, and Agatha liked him for politely hiding the contempt which she imagined any intellectual must have for so hideous a room.

'I should imagine you don't have a very amusing time here,' he said sympathetically.

'No, it's very dull. Nothing to do but read or go to the cinema.'

'That's the case with so many people in this wretched war. One's youth is wasted. I shall be joining the Army soon.'

'Do you enjoy it at Oxford?'

'Yes, on the whole, it's very pleasant.'

Agatha tried to find out about his life there, but he seemed to be more interested in her. She was horrified at how little she had to tell him about herself, and soon found herself magnifying the smallest incidents into 'stories' with which she hoped to amuse him. She made out that a young man, to whom she had actually only spoken once or twice at a party, had tried to make love to her, and enlarged on her imaginary difficulties in getting rid of him. 'For God's sake don't tell Mother,' she ended up, 'or she'd have kittens.'

'Yes, you must have a troop of admirers after you,' he said, sitting down next to her on a sofa.

'But they're so awfully dull, Philip,' she said, turning to him. 'Why Mother insists on remaining in this provincial place I can't imagine. Sometimes I think I'll write a book about it all.'

'You really ought to. You're lucky to have such good copy near at hand.'

They started to talk about books, and from then on any strain there might have been between them disappeared. Agatha's confidence returned; Philip was not, she decided, as clever as he thought himself, but she did not like him less for this. They discovered a mutual taste for jazz music, and Agatha played him her small selection of records.

'I hardly ever get a chance to put them on,' she said.

'You really must come and stay with us next summer,' he said. 'I've got some records you'd like. I wish to goodness I'd brought them with me, but I never thought I'd find an enthusiast here.'

'I suppose you thought I'd be madly boring.'

Unequal to this, he showed his embarrassment, and muttered, 'Of course not.'

'I'd simply love to come. I want to see your books, too.'

'I'll send you that book on Proust. Remind me before I leave.'

Herself reminded by this that he was supposed to be staying a week, Agatha said, 'I'm afraid you'll be terribly bored here.'

He smiled at her. 'Oh, we'll find some amusing things to do, I'm sure, Agatha.'

But even as he said this, she could see that her remark had taken effect, and wished that she had never uttered it.

Eventually he said, 'How long is it till tea?'

'Quarter of an hour. Are you starving?'

'No, but if you don't mind I think I'll go upstairs and dash off a letter. I should have written it yesterday.'

She watched him leave the room, and then began to gather up the gramophone records which were scattered over the floor. She was happy, even looking forward to Mrs Lyddiard's return from the lecture. Her interest in Philip had revived her affection for her mother; as soon as she knew herself appreciated by someone, she could forget the misunderstandings and boredom which up till then had seemed to permeate her home life.

After tea, Agatha left Mrs Lyddiard with Philip in the drawing-room, and went upstairs to do the black-out in the bedrooms. Her mother had irritated her at tea, repeating too often how nice it was for Agatha to have someone of her own age in the house at last, and also that it seemed only yesterday when Philip had been a baby in arms. Agatha sensed that Philip disliked having attention thus drawn to his youth; he was conscious, and proud, of sophistication.

The gloom of evening filled the landing; the Cries of London were dark smudges on the walls. She turned first of all into her own room. This had an empty, impersonal air about it, in spite of the dark wall-paper and solid furniture, for Agatha's occupation of it was indicated only by a novel by Virginia Woolf and

66

a photograph of Gary Cooper on the dressing-table. She did not linger there.

Her mother's bedroom was a mass of photographs; the faces of many friends and relations, and, above all, her mother's own, snapped at every stage of its career, glared at Agatha when she switched on the light. The frames were ornate, with the exception of one containing a recent photograph of Agatha herself; this was plain, made of glass and steel, and the face inside it looked naked and immature. Having drawn the heavy curtains, Agatha, still for a moment, could just hear voices in the drawing-room below, and wondered what was being said.

The spare room was furnished like the others; the patterns on the wallpaper and china jug and basin were florid, the chest of drawers and wardrobe were menacing in the half-light. Philip had laid out his striped woollen pyjamas on the bed and his sponge bag dangled from the basin, but otherwise his luggage was still unpacked. Agatha noticed a stamped and addressed envelope on the dressing-table; picking it up with curiosity she saw that the flap had not yet been stuck. Unable to resist the temptation of learning more about the young man who was filling her thoughts, she carefully extracted the letter within. He had left her, she remembered, to 'dash this off' before tea. The notepaper was her mother's, with the address printed at the top. Beneath was written in neat classical handwriting,

'Dear Derek,

You will wonder what I am doing at the above address. Well, I am staying a week with a godmother, in a Gothic revival villa in a very genteel suburb. The godmother, however, seems kind if a bit over-bearing, and the villa is comfortable in an old-fashioned sort of way. There is also a daughter, who seems intelligent, although much too intense – she has just reached the Aldous Huxley stage! She's a year younger than me; rather beautiful, but her clothes are too arty, very Slade school, which is probably her intention. I feel I could do something here (I have just been tête-à-tête with her all afternoon, and the mother is always leaving us alone together), but the thought of a romantic friendship in this atmosphere is really too oppressive, so I shall probably keep her at bay. This sounds very conceited and unchivalrous, but I wouldn't write like this to anyone but you.

Will I see you at Oxford next term? I very much want to read you the last chapters of the book, I am rather pleased with them. Your opinion will be invaluable.

Must rush now, I have just realised that a terrible din which has been going on for some time is the maid beating the Indian gong for tea! Do write soon.

Philip.

P.S. Better not write here, I doubt if I can stick it for a week. Write to Walton Street.'

Agatha stood for a moment motionless after reading this. Then she quickly and carefully replaced the letter in the envelope, and when she was satisfied that her interference would not be noticed, she left the room.

Going downstairs, she met Philip coming up.

'Just going out to stretch my legs and post a letter,' he said as they passed each other. She joined her mother in the drawing-room.

'This is our first opportunity to discuss our guest,' said Mrs Lyddiard.

'Be careful, he might hear,' said Agatha in a low voice. She picked up her Huxley book, and then put it down again. They heard Philip run downstairs, and shut the front door behind him.

'He's a dear boy, don't you think?' said Mrs Lyddiard.

'Yes, he's rather nice.'

Mrs Lyddiard looked arch. 'Now, Agatha, tell me, honest injun, do you think he's attractive?'

Agatha turned to her mother, her eyes limpid, her expression puzzled.

'Attractive? No, I can't say I do. Of course, I suppose he might be to some people, in a puppy-ish sort of way. But after all, Mother, he is so very young.'

Iris Metcalfe

THE PIANO LESSON

THIS story begins at half past nine one summer morning, in the broad main street of a market town.

Outside the Town Hall at one end of the street there was a notice advertising a Whist Drive to take place there that evening, and another, recently printed at the offices of the *Norford Gazette*, which read: 'The Norford Amateur Dramatic and Operatic Society present two performances of *The Midshipmaid*, on July 10th and 17th at 7.0 p.m. in the Town Hall. Tickets to be obtained from Mrs Metcalfe, "Kalipur", Buckingham Road, and from the *Norford Gazette*, High Street.'

Women were walking along the pavements and in and out of the shops which had been open an hour: large red Woolworths, popular for the snack counter at the back of the shop where tasteless hard lumps of vanilla ice cream were sold, balanced at the top of wafer cones; its nearby rival, green Marks and Spencers; the blue front of the Violet Tea Rooms; the streamlined Court Hairdresser, with neat heads in the window advertising Evan Williams Shampoo and the Marcel Wave; black, gloomy Freeman Hardy & Willis, displaying behind a smooth window-pane a multitude of court shoes; Boots Cash Chemist, and the gay, monogrammic sign of W. H. Smith & Son dangling above a window in which were piled many copies of a new book with a local interest, called *Norford Rambles*.

Outside W. H. Smith's there stood a queue of people waiting for a bus. Some of them were altering their wrist-watches to the time told by the Church clock, which was, confusingly, ten minutes later than that on the clock of the Town Hall tower opposite. The bus appeared, a long red single-decker with its rows of jolting heads which, on entering the town, all turned outward to present to the pavements their pale, unrecognisable faces. The bus slowly circled the street, and then stopped reluctantly at the queue, in exactly the right position, so that the woman at the head of the queue found herself just at the entrance to the bus. This woman had to wait, with increasing impatience, while the former passengers climbed out.

The last two people to leave the bus were a little girl of eight and a middle-aged woman, her governess. Mary jumped out on to the pavement, but Miss Hunt took her time over the two steps, and then stood for a moment at the bottom, breathing heavily, as though she had just stepped from a dark room into one dazzlingly light.

'Don't be such a slowcoach, Miss Hunt,' said Mary. 'We've only got ten minutes to shop in before the lesson.'

She walked on impatiently, pushing past the other shoppers in the street, and the governess followed, moving with precision, while the bus filled with its new load and the driver and conductor disappeared into the Violet for a quick cup of coffee.

Miss Hunt's purchases took place in a small, dark, draper's shop in a street leading out of the High Street, uphill, towards the common. In its window stood two models, one of which represented a smiling woman with smooth brown hair, on whom was hung a green summer dress; its price dangled from one of the arched slim fingers, each carefully separated from the other. The second model was a schoolboy with red cheeks and sturdy legs; he wore a cap and blazer and grey trousers which reached below his knees.

Inside the shop one tired assistant waited behind the counter. Rolls of material were piled together, and some stuffs were draped against the white boxes which stood along the walls. The smell of the shop made Mary think of Miss Hunt's underclothes.

Miss Hunt bought some buttons, some hooks and eyes, some thin knitting needles and some material with a dark green pattern on a pale green background. The material, which was not for herself, but for her sister who lived in Reading, was measured out in yards by the assistant, cut, folded and covered to form a neat brown paper parcel with impressive competence.

Then Miss Hunt and Mary walked on up the hill, Miss Hunt with her parcels and Mary with a portfolio containing sheet music, for she had come into Norford to have her piano lesson.

The houses in Buckingham Road which faced the common

(on which this morning a group of children were playing round-
ers) were detached, and each had a little garden and a garage
shaded by laurels. Each had steps leading up to the front door,
and a large window on the ground floor. They were built of
grey stone; at the back, they each had a glass conservatory. One
or two, larger than the others, were built so as to resemble
miniature castles, with two square towers and little chinks in
the stone which were the servants' windows. Most of them had
some sign on the garden gate; one belonged to a doctor, another
to a dentist; one was a school of typing and shorthand, and
another the headquarters of the YWCA.

'Kalipur' had no sign on its gate. It belonged to Mrs
Metcalfe, the widow of an assistant master at the public school
just outside the town, and for which it was well known; she
lived there with her daughter Iris, who was to give Mary her
piano lesson.

Mary followed her governess through the gate of 'Kalipur'
and along the crazy pavement in the middle of which was a
chipped stone bird bath. On either side of the front door, and
above it, were panes of stained glass. When the door was suddenly opened, just as Miss Hunt was reaching for the knocker,
they could see that the sun shining through the fanlight lit part
of the floor in the dark hall and coloured it, as oil does a puddle
in the street.

Mrs Metcalfe had opened the door. She was a large, energetic
woman, between fifty and sixty. She was pulling a shapeless
hat down over her grey curls, beneath which swung green ear-
rings. She was smoking a cigarette.

'Oh, good morning. Isn't it a heavenly day? Quite God-given.
It seems a shame you should have to stuff indoors at the piano.
I'll call Iris, I don't know where she's got to. Iris!' She sang this
name, for Mrs Metcalfe had a contralto voice. 'I've just written
a note to your mother,' she said to Mary. 'She's behind with her
subscription to the Conservative Society. One has to pester
people when one is held responsible. Just wait in the drawing-
room till Iris comes down. Heaven knows what she's doing.'
She walked out into the garden, calling up to a first-floor window,
'Iris, little Mary Stone is here, don't keep her waiting.' A faint
voice could be heard from upstairs: 'Coming, Mummy.'

Miss Hunt put her parcels down on the umbrella stand in
the hall beneath the barometer which hung on the wall. Mary

71

removed her hat and gloves. Then they went into the drawing-room.

In spite of the big window, this room was dark and oppressive. It contained a heavy roll-top writing-table, on which were an inkstand, pens, a blotter, sealing-wax, a pen-wiper and several tradesmen's calendars. There were many photographs in the room, most of them school groups or portraits of pupils of the late Mr Metcalfe, presented to him on their leaving school. On them were written such inscriptions as 'To G.L.M. from P.H. 1924-30'. In the middle of the room there was a big table with magazines on it. There was a bookcase with glass doors which looked as if it were never opened; and, indeed, it never was, because the doors had been locked and the key mislaid. In one corner stood an old, upright piano, with yellow notes. A fringed shawl had been placed on the top, and on that there was a bowl of ferns. The music stand was bent sideways, forming a complicated zig-zag pattern; on either side of it projected a candlestick. Beside the piano was a music rack containing music neatly arranged.

While the two visitors stood in the drawing-room, they heard Mrs Metcalfe start up her two-seater which they later saw move slowly past the window. They could see her, a cigarette still in her mouth, leaning over the steering wheel and staring through the windscreen at the road.

Miss Hunt said in the restrained voice which she used in other people's houses, 'Why don't you start practising?' She looked about her with an air of disapproval.

Mary went over to the piano stool, which she adjusted to suit her own height. Then she took from her portfolio a book of music called 'Off we Go!' and, opening the piano, began to play a piece in it called 'Ronde'. She looked all the time at her hands, and never at the music, because she could not sight-read, and had to learn a piece by heart before she could play it at all. For some reason the tune which she knew so well sounded more professional and convincing on this piano than it did when Mary played it on the one at her home. When she pressed the loud pedal, she could hear it shift somewhere inside the instrument. Mary wondered why pianists did not play with the loud pedal on all the time.

Miss Metcalfe's system was to make her pupils practise one week the right-hand part of a piece, the next week the left-hand,

and the third week the two together. Thus they all moved at an equal pace through 'Off we Go!' and the more advanced books which succeeded it. A friend of Mary's, who had started a fortnight before her, was therefore always one piece ahead of her, and Mary hoped that Susan would one day be ill, so that Mary would be able to catch her up, and perhaps even pass her in the steady race. At the moment Mary was the youngest, and most backward, of the pupils. At Miss Metcalfe's annual concert, when they performed to an audience consisting of their parents, Mary was always the first to play. This was the final week to be devoted to 'Ronde', and if the teacher was satisfied with Mary's performance, she was to start today on the right hand part of the following tune, which was called 'Berceuse'.

It was rare for a piano lesson to be conducted at 'Kalipur'; Miss Metcalfe preferred to borrow her mother's car and visit her pupils, no doubt owing to the inferiority of her own piano. Today the car had been needed by Mrs Metcalfe, and so Mary had travelled the five miles from her house in the bus.

Miss Hunt selected a *Sporting and Dramatic* from the magazines on the table, and sat down stiffly on a leather armchair. She turned immediately to the Dramatic section, but then she realised that she had already seen this edition, and so she picked out a *Country Life* instead.

Iris Metcalfe came into the room, smiling apologetically. She was a tall woman of thirty, with a big white face and brown hair arranged in a nondescript manner. She wore a summer dress made of much the same material as that just bought by Miss Hunt for her sister; her arms were thin and pale, and the bare elbows wrinkled. Iris was usually seen in the company of her mother, whose personality was strong enough to obliterate Iris's altogether. When not with her mother, any sign of initiative on Iris's part, any individual movement or spontaneous sentence, was as surprising, and as endearing, as a child's remark whose influence cannot be easily traced.

Iris brought up a chair to the piano, and sat by while Mary played her piece. Mary was depressed by the smell of her teacher's clothes and hair, and the sight of her broad, clumsy, hands which were suddenly nimble when at the piano.

While the lesson was in progress, Miss Hunt laid down her magazine, and after a pause began a conversation.

'Have you had any news of Mr Metcalfe?'

This referred to Iris's brother Alan, who was a year or two older than her; he had a stutter, and was abroad.

'Not for some time. Are you coming to the Drive tonight, Miss Hunt?'

Iris talked to Miss Hunt, watching Mary's fingers all the time, and occasionally interrupting the adult conversation to say, 'Not so much pedal, Mary,' or to groan humorously and grimace when the child struck a wrong note.

'I don't see how I'm to manage it,' answered Miss Hunt. 'I can get a bus to take me in, but I can't get a bus to take me back. Will you be there?'

'No, I've given up going, but Mummy's giving the prizes.'

'Oh, and what has she chosen?' asked Miss Hunt, with some hesitation, as though the question were an indelicate one; and so it may have been, for Iris answered with a careless air of deprecation, 'The men's prizes are all cigarettes, I believe. She's got rather a jolly Ladies' First Prize though; an ebony shoehorn, with glove stretchers to match. I tell her I'm tempted to play myself, just to try and win it! The Ladies' Second Prize is a pair of shoe trees. She's just gone out to see if she can get a suitable Consolation anywhere – a vase, we thought, or something of the sort.'

'How very nice.'

Mary, bored with the conversation, and wishing to attract attention, now struck an exaggerated discord; Iris said, 'Mary! You can't be concentrating. That sounded fearful.'

Mary found an opportunity to repeat a favourite catch phrase: 'Beg your pardon, Mrs Arden, there's a chicken in your garden.'

'I say, Miss Hunt, I shall have to buy a little bat, and hit her over the knuckles whenever she makes a mistake. She'd make far less then, I'm sure.'

Mary giggled, and her governess said crossly, 'She can play it correctly if she wants to, but she doesn't try.' Then, after waiting a little, she continued the interrupted conversation with Iris. 'The last time I came in to a Norford Drive, there were so many more ladies than men, that I had to play as a man, if you know what I mean. I obtained the highest score in the room, but of course I had to have the Men's First Prize – forty Gold Flake cigarettes, which were no good to me, as I don't smoke. However, I sent them to my brother, and he was very pleased with them.'

Mary, who had heard this story many times, was wondering what a Whist Drive could be like. She knew how to play Whist, but the word 'Drive' suggested something more exciting, and she longed to know exactly what it meant.

Miss Hunt continued, 'Oh, before I forget it, Mrs Stone asked me to ask you when and where the next rehearsal is.'

'Here, on Saturday afternoon; I do hope she turns up, and knows her part. I'm stage-managing, you know.'

'I'm sure we're all very much looking forward to the performance. They are always so amusing. It must be hard work.'

'Oh, there's masses to do. But I prefer it to acting.'

'I'm sorry you haven't a part.'

'Goodness,' said Iris, turning from the piano and pulling at the rings on her fingers, 'I can't act for toffee-apples. What I do do keeps me busy enough. I have to get the play typed out, and send copies to everyone, with all their speeches marked in pencil. And I have to get hold of all the scenery, and see people turn up at rehearsals.'

Mary, who had turned her head away during this speech and had been picking her nose, now slipped off the stool and went up to Miss Hunt, whispering something in her ear.

'May I take her upstairs, Miss Metcalfe?'

'Of course. You know the way.'

Iris waited standing until they returned. The lesson was over. 'You must let us hear *you* before we leave,' said Miss Hunt.

So Iris sat down again at the piano and played a 'Song Without Words' while the governess tried to prevent Mary from fidgeting, and whispering, 'We'll miss the bus.'

When at last they were putting on their coats in the hall, they could smell food and hear the dining-room table being laid for lunch. The sound of Iris playing by herself followed them down Buckingham Road, and as they turned downhill they passed Mrs Metcalfe in her car, squinting ahead of her and clutching the steering wheel with determination.

THE GRAMOPHONE CLUB

The shops had shut for the lunch hour, but now they were opening again. Iris walked along the High Street to the Town Hall, which she entered by a side door. Tables, with four chairs at each, were set on the floor in preparation for the Whist Drive; they were covered in green baize, and on each had been placed a pack of cards and a marker with pencil attached. Iris knew well the formula of these entertainments; the chatter while at each table the hands were dealt, the hush while the cards were picked up and hastily arranged, fanlike, in their suits, the sporadic talk and laughter while the game was played. After each hand, the winning man moved up (for every table was numbered, by a chalk mark on the baize), the winning lady down, and the losing couple stayed at the same table, only altering their positions so that they no longer faced each other. The proceeds of the Drive went to the Women's Institute, of which Mrs Metcalfe was Treasurer, and Miriam Holmes, Secretary.

Miriam was now standing on the stage in the hall, talking to an electrician in a blue overall. She was arranging about the lighting for *The Midshipmaid*, which she was producing, and in which she was taking the leading part. Miriam was the daughter of a Norford housemaster; she was Iris's greatest friend, and Iris admired her, because she ran the local Pony Club, and had a hand in every club or Institute formed in the town. Miriam was the same age as Iris, whom she had known all her life; she had bright red hair and a pale, freckled, face.

'I'll be with you in a moment, darling,' she called.

Iris sat down at one of the tables, and looked about the hall. She had seen it arranged in many different ways; as today, for a Whist Drive; as it would shortly be, with the chairs in rows and facing the stage in front of which a curtain would precariously be hung, for the amateur dramatics; and, as on every Saturday night, with the floor cleared and the chairs along the walls, ready for the weekly dance. On these occasions, the local band was hired, and sat on the stage playing from seven o'clock till ten. They advertised themselves as 'Bert Collins and his Boys, Playing Music in the Modern Manner'. If the band had a previous engagement, the man from Powell's Gramophone Shop brought a radiogram to the hall, standing by it on the stage and announcing each dance before playing one of his limited supply of records. Iris imagined she could hear him now : 'Ladies and Gentlemen, take your partners for the Valeta!' Or the Paul Jones, the Tango, the Waltz, the Foxtrot and the Quickstep . . .

76

The electrician went away, and Miriam stepped down from the stage. 'Sorry to keep you . . .' she looked at her wrist-watch. 'We'll have to hurry, or we'll be late.'

Miriam picked up a pile of gramophone records which she had placed on one of the tables, and Iris followed her out of the hall. Miriam handed the records to Iris when they were outside, and turned round to lock the door behind her. Then she wriggled her shoulders under her cotton dress, and holding out her hands for the records said, 'Wouldn't it be nice to go for a swim today?'

They took a turning off the High Street, uphill, in the opposite direction to that leading up to the common, for the town lay in a valley. Miriam said, 'My dear, I'm counting on you to accompany my 'cello solo for the school concert.'

'Will there be many people this afternoon?'

'I doubt it. Some of the school are really awfully keen but it takes a lot of persuading to get them to try something new. Of course if nobody comes I shall have to give it up.'

'Tell me,' said Iris, 'have you met a new master called Mr Hill? Mother said at lunch that she'd asked him to tea today.'

'The Science man? My dear, yes, he's rather sweet. He came to dinner the other day, and sang. He's got a gorgeous voice.'

'That will give me something to talk to him about at tea.' Iris imagined herself saying later that afternoon, 'I hear you sing, Mr Hill.' 'How do you know that, Miss Metcalfe?' an agreeable tenor voice would enquire; and she would say, 'A little bird told me.' But no doubt Mrs Metcalfe would ask him to sing, before she had the chance.

They had now reached the outskirts of the town, where the school buildings began. Out of breath, they stopped for a moment to watch the bowling at the nets. A thin-haired master, wearing light grey flannels and a blue blazer with gold buttons, stood in the middle of a cricket field holding a bat and ball, surrounded by a widespread circle of schoolboys.

'There's Daddy taking fielding-practice,' said Miriam.

The master sent the ball high up into the air; Iris watched it ascend, dizzy, until her eyes watered and she lost it; the fielders were standing tense, their heads upturned; suddenly the ball was again visible, descending fast; Iris jumped nervously as one of the fielders placed himself beneath it, hands cupped; the hands received it, and he jerked them back between his open knees, but the ball jumped out, fell and rolled along the ground. The other boys groaned and the master said crossly, 'What's the matter with you, Schofield?' Schofield smiled uneasily.

'Come on,' said Miriam. She led Iris into the gymnasium.

The ropes were looped up and fastened to the handle-bars that stood along the walls, to leave the room clear. In one corner were gathered together two jumping-horses, some footballs, and a pile of long poles. Iris wondered what the poles were for. An electric radiogram stood at one end of the room, plugged into a light that hung from the ceiling. Round this were grouped two schoolboys and an elderly woman dressed in a uniform not unlike that of a hospital nurse.

'Matron,' shouted Miriam, in her irritatingly piercing voice, 'how splendid of you to come!'

'I heard there was to be music, Miss Holmes, and I never miss a concert if I can help it.'

'Is this everybody then?' asked Miriam.

One of the boys, who was very fat, said in a cultured voice, 'It's not a very good attendance, but alas, many who wanted to were unable to come. Schofield was mad keen – his aunt plays professionally, you know, she was on the wireless the other night – but he couldn't get out of fielding practice.'

'Oh dear. But four people is better than nothing.'

Iris glanced at the other boy, who was good-looking and wore a sulky, embarrassed expression. Then she looked through an open door near the gramophone, which led into a small room in which a PT instructor was punching a ball attached to the ceiling. The room was full of photographs of boxers and wrestlers. The instructor was small, and wore only a pair of blue trousers, secured by elastic round the waist, and tucked at the bottom into black boots. His muscular arms were covered with tattoo-marks. Suddenly he picked up a rugger ball, put it under his arm, and ran through the gymnasium and out of it, without looking at the others.

Matron sucked in her cheeks and looked round her with a smile. 'Where are we all to sit? Personally, I think the floor looks a bit hard.'

'Oh dear, there aren't any chairs. I never thought of that, wasn't I dippy? Could you two boys be poppets and run and secure us some form of seat? Anything would do, we can't 'afford to be choosy, but some deck chairs would be jolly if you could find any.'

'No sooner said than done. We won't be half a mo.'

Iris noticed a pile of hairy mats in one corner, the kind that are placed in front of a jumping-horse, for the jumper to land on. 'Couldn't we lie on those?' she said.

'Darling, what a brain wave. Let's drag them out.'

'Very luxurious and restful,' said Matron, uncertainly.

'A bit hairy,' said the fat boy. 'They're inclined to tickle but we might try.'

The boys dragged four of the mats into the middle of the room and put them side by side, facing the gramophone. Then the fat boy lay on one, resting his head on his hands. 'Very comfy,' he said.

'Splendid,' said Matron, sitting down gingerly. 'Yes, this will do splendidly.' Iris sat next to her, leaning on one elbow on which was soon imprinted the mat hairs' pattern. The good-looking boy lay down flat on her other side, staring up at the ceiling.

'Well,' said Miriam, 'now we can start.' She cleared her throat. 'The first record I've chosen is a Paul Robeson, because I know he's always popular. Singing,' she squinted at the label, 'the "Eriskay Love Lilt ".'

'Wizard.'

Miriam switched on the gramophone, changed the needle, and started the record. Then, with exaggerated caution, she tiptoed back to the mats, and lowered herself to the ground, wincing slightly as the rough hairs touched her cotton dress. The fat boy listened with an expression of strained intelligence on his white, good-humoured face; Matron squatted by him, her mouth serene, her eyes preoccupied; Iris looked down at the other boy, who had closed his eyes. Suddenly she thought, 'How much younger he is than me.'

As a child, she had looked forward to the beginning of term with excitement, as it meant the presence of straw-hatted youths in the town, some of whom she knew. But she never knew one for longer than six years, as once they reached the interesting age of nineteen, and often sooner, they left the school and never came back. As a young girl this excitement had deepened to a more urgent sensation, for she had felt that her social life depended entirely on the schoolboys. Now she realised that for some time they had seemed children to her; she was the contemporary of the masters now, no longer that of the pupils. Iris felt sure that she would never get used to that idea.

The record ended. Miriam stayed motionless for a moment, as if still listening to the song; then she noticed that the needle was scratching on the inner circle of the record, and she rose to change it.

'What a voice,' said Matron, altering her uncomfortable position with relief.

'Do let's have the other side,' said the fat boy, his face gleaming with enjoyment.

'I don't know whether we have time. I want to get in the whole of the D minor concerto if I can before Abbers, and you don't want to be late for that. If we do have time, I'll play it at the end.'

'D minor concerto?' said Matron. 'I had heard a rumour that we were to have the Jupiter.'

'I hope you don't mind,' said Miriam, 'but I thought the D minor might be more popular.'

'Oh, delightful, but I must confess a soft spot for the Jupiter.'

Iris lay back and closed her eyes when the Mozart began. Her hip was just touching that of the good-looking boy; she checked an impulse to move, deciding to wait and see if he would. He did not, however, and soon she ceased to notice his proximity.

The sun shone through the high windows on to the smooth floorboards. Iris wondered which of her private imaginary scenes she would choose to accompany the music. She decided on her favourite.

There she was, sitting somewhere at the back of a crowded concert hall in Wigmore Street. She was clapping the conductor, (at first a shadowy figure, until she determined on his identity; today he would be Sir Malcolm Sargent). The orchestra had finished tuning up. There was an excited silence in the auditorium while Sir Malcolm walked towards the wings and held out his hand to someone lurking there. Faces stared at the stage and hands rustled programmes on laps. An old lady next to Iris put on her glasses and stared at her programme which she was holding upside down. 'What comes now?' she muttered. 'Mozart's piano concerto in D minor,' Iris whispered. 'Who's the soloist?' 'Look, there she is!' Sir Malcolm led on to the stage a tall girl in a white evening dress with neat brown hair and ear-rings like Mrs Metcalfe's. 'Isn't she good-looking?' said the old lady. 'Who is she?' 'Iris Metcalfe.' 'Ah, yes.' The Iris in the audience clapped loudly while the Iris on the stage bowed, with a smile, first to the spectators and then to Sir Malcolm. When the clapping stopped, moving deliberately and slowly, the soloist walked towards the enormous piano. She adjusted the stool and flexed her fingers. Then she exchanged a look, over her shoulder, with the conductor.

Lying on the mat in the gymnasium, Iris was excited by this imaginary scene. She was holding her breath and clenching her hands. What a moment! Then, returning to consciousness, she wondered: When will it happen? She opened her eyes and decided, Never. But that did not matter, for the scene took place in her imagination, no doubt far more pleasantly than it would in real life, every time she listened to a piano concerto. She had no regret, on waking up, that her dream was only a dream, for she knew that the dream was an improvement on actuality.

The last record over, Miriam said, 'I think we've time for the Robeson again, if you'd care to hear it.'

Iris rose. 'I must go home now,' she said in a shaking voice. 'I mustn't be late for tea. Don't get up,' she said to the boys who had made no move.

'Tomorrow morning for coffee at the Violet, don't forget,' said Miriam, turning to the gramophone.

Outside in the sun Iris blinked as she walked lightly downhill to the town.

TEA

When she reached 'Kalipur', out of breath and sweating after her hot walk, Iris noticed a green pork-pie hat, with a pheasant's feather stuck in the brim, hanging in the hall. She held her breath, and could distinguish a man's voice mingling with her mother's loud deep one in the conversation coming from the drawing-room. She went quickly into the room known as her father's study.

The bookshelves here contained a collection of Loeb classics and many old school books: Latin Primers, edited copies of *Julius Caesar* and *The Merchant of Venice*, Caesar's *Gallic War*.

These were heavily marked in ink, and bore on their fly-leaves the names of the different schoolboys who had at various times owned them. Iris imagined she could smell in the study the tobacco which Mr Metcalfe had smoked, and, although he had been dead some years, it was still very much his room. It was here that, dribbling along his pipe-stem, a loose tweed mountain sunk in the swivel-chair behind his desk, he had received the group of boys who, every Thursday evening, had come stumbling out of the dark to be prepared, unwillingly, for Confirmation.

Iris stood in the study and wondered how she would make her entrance into the drawing-room. Somehow she must penetrate into the room – unless she went to bed with a headache? Her curiosity about Mr Hill, however, decided her against this. Should she slink in, creep in, stalk in, swing in, burst in . . .? Her mother's voice called angrily, 'Iris! What on earth are you doing?' She hurried out of the study repeating her usual obedient phrase, 'Coming, Mummy,' and found herself in the drawing-room before she realised it.

Her mother was sitting behind the teapot, opposite a man who clumsily rose from his chair when Iris came in.

'This is my daughter Iris, Mr Hill,' said Mrs Metcalfe in a bored way, as though she wished to get the introduction over as soon as possible. Iris held out her hand, staring at the stranger but, owing to a nervousness which she always felt on meeting someone new, unable to distinguish his features or receive any impression of his appearance. Mr Hill also held out his hand, but wide of Iris's, and as both leaned forward they missed each other, and nearly poked each other in the stomach. Iris giggled nervously, and there was an agitated movement of hands, until finally Mr Hill captured two of Iris's limp fingers and shook them heartily with a large red hand on which grew pale hairs.

'Sit down, Iris, and drink your tea. I'm afraid it's stewed, but that's your look out, if you must be late for meals.'

Iris sat down miserably, wishing that her mother would not treat her as though she were twenty years younger than she was. She found it difficult, when spoken to as a child of ten, not to answer in that character – sulkily, saucily or precociously – and thus appear ridiculous. Mrs Melcafe, as though a tiresome interruption were now over, turned with a charming smile to her guest. Iris sipped her tea (which was indeed very dark, and tepid) and studied Mr Hill.

He was tall and thin, and wore a light-grey flannel suit, a white shirt and an Old Norfordian tie. His sandy hair appeared to be thick, as it was wiry and stood up in a wall above his white forehead, but in fact it was sparsely distributed over his head, and was already thinning at the crown. His face was pale and lightly freckled, and Iris suddenly noticed the beginnings of a soft moustache on his upper lip. He may have seen her look at it, for he said now, 'I have always been clean-shaven up to now, but on coming to Norford I decided I was altogether too mild-looking to keep a class in order, so I started this moustache in the hope of frightening the boys. I'm rather pleased with it,' he said, stroking it with a slightly facetious air. 'I call it Bertram.'

Iris smiled, and her mother screamed out a laugh, saying, 'How perfectly priceless!'

'How do you like it at Norford?' Iris asked timidly. Her mother looked angry and embarrassed, as she often did when Iris spoke in public, giving the impression that her daughter was not quite all there, and might at any moment say something wild and obscene. She quickly interrupted, before Mr Hill could answer, and indeed before anyone could be sure that he had heard Iris's question, 'Isn't it splendid to think that the summer holidays will soon be here? Where do you go? When my husband was alive we always went to Switzerland, but since his death we have only visited friends in this country. It isn't the same as abroad.'

With a clatter Iris replaced her cup and saucer on the table. The presence of a stranger put her off her appetite. When people came to tea, she liked to eat nothing at the meal, but later to go into the kitchen and finish the drop-scones by herself.

Mr Hill's pale grey eyes sparkled at his hostess's question, and he leant forward. 'Oh, I had a capital holiday a few years ago. An experience I shall never forget. I made a trek to the Passion Play at Oberammergau.'

Iris forgot her diffidence, and said with interest, 'It lasts for days, doesn't it? And they all wear their own beards?'

'Oh, yes, no one could possibly take offence at the presentation of,' he lowered his voice, 'our Lord on the stage, it is all so natural and reverent and moving.'

'Like *The Miracle*, or *Everyman*,' said Mrs Metcalfe.

'But Oberammergau is in a class by itself. Here, I have some photos.'

Mr Hill drew a wallet from his inside pocket, and from that some postcards of scenes from the passion play. The two women leant forward, breath held in reverence, and did not know what to say. Each felt that if the other had not been there, she would have said something suitable, interesting and original, and made a friend of the schoolmaster.

After a time Mr Hill tucked the photographs back into his pocket. He turned to Iris, who received his attention with a frightened face, and said, 'Your mother tells me that I am among a musical family.'

She answered in a little rush, accenting the wrong words like a foreigner and avoiding her mother's face on which she could imagine a gathering frown, 'Yes, Mummy sings awfully nicely.'

'And you play?'

'After a fashion.'

'Nonsense,' said Mrs Metcalfe. 'Don't be so modest, you know you play very well. Not first class, perhaps, not even second – you know your own limitations, but within them,' she said, turning to the man, 'she is quite an artist. We sent her to the Royal College when we saw she had talent.'

'I should love to hear you – if I might,' said Mr Hill humbly. Iris was thinking, 'If only Mummy were not here, I could talk about music, get his ideas on my favourite composers, and he would like me. But what I want to say comes out differently when she's there. Please God make her be called to the telephone.'

'Iris,' said Mrs Metcalfe (in a tone which implied, 'Here is your chance, at last, for heaven's sake wake up and take it'), 'why don't you accompany Mr Hill in a song?'

'You sing?' said Iris, with assumed surprise.

'Not today, alas. I've been laid up with a septic throat, so it's out of the question.'

'Play that charming sea thing – Macdowell, or whatever the man's name is,' continued Mrs Metcalfe, like an enormous engine which nothing can stop. 'Go on.'

'Oh, no Mummy, I'm sure Mr Hill wouldn't care for that.'

'Well, play something, child, Mr Hill doesn't want to wait all night,' said Mrs Melcalfe, turning to the man with an amused, sympathetic expression.

'If Miss Metcalfe would rather not,' began the visitor, looking at his wrist-watch in evident embarrassment.

'Of course she wants to,' said Mrs Metcalfe sharply. 'What's the use of having a talent if you have to be begged and entreated to use it? It's mock modesty,' she said angrily, and then smiled, to show that she was not really angry, and added softly, 'That's all it is.'

In the following silence Iris found herself obliged to speak. 'I'd rather not play today,' she said, as firmly as she could. She had been ready, had indeed wanted to play to Mr Hill, but the long, embarrassing discussion had numbed, not only her fingers, but her whole body, so that she felt incapable of reaching the piano, let alone of playing it.

Mrs Metcalfe twitched her shoulders, and, avoiding looking at her daughter, turned to the schoolmaster with an apologetic expression, as though asking his forgiveness for her dog which had bitten him, and hoping that he would like her herself none the less after the incident, for which she had been only partly responsible.

Iris stood up. She longed to say something to Mr Hill, but through a strange wilfulness she ignored her hatred of her mother, which had been increasing during the last few minutes, and addressed her with an affectionate smile. 'Now I'm going to leave for Devizes,' she said.

Mr Hill looked surprised. 'You'll have a long journey in front of you,' he said.

Mrs Metcalfe shouted with laughter. 'Priceless! No, my dear man, Iris didn't mean what she said. It's a family joke. All the nicest families have family jokes, don't you think? I'm sure yours has. You see, my husband had an old Aunt Emma – she's been dead for years – but she was very deaf. One day she was in here and I had to go out, so I said to her, "Now, I'm going to leave you to your own devices". After I'd gone, Gerald came in, and said "Where's Clarice, Aunt Emma?" And Aunt Emma said, "She's just left for Devizes!" You see, she hadn't heard me correctly.'

'So after that,' said Iris, 'whenever one of us goes off somewhere, we always say, "Now I'm going to leave for Devizes".'

After a short pause, Mr Hill said 'Capital!' and, throwing his head back and his legs out, and hitting his knee with his hand, laughed for a long time. It seemed to Iris that some of his

laughter was false, and that he was not as amused as he pretended. She slipped out of the room before he had finished
laughing. She walked slowly up the carpeted stairs, dragging
her feet, and entered her own bedroom. She sat down on the
brown and beige-striped counterpane which covered the narrow
bed. Above the bed there hung, and had hung for twenty years,
a flat cardboard spaniel, with 'Doggie' lettered in gold along
the bottom. There were several calendars nailed to the fidgety
wallpaper. The room was very neat, for Iris had a mania for
tidiness, and hid every article she possessed in the chest of
drawers; inside the drawers, however, all was confusion.

Some time ago, Iris had seen in a copy of a magazine called
Prediction, lent to her by Miriam, the following advertisement:

'Madame Marianne Robinson-Williams, Spiritual Medium.
Numerology, psychometry, astrology, clairvoyance, Inspira-
tional messages, herbs, faith healing. Send birth date and 5/-
P.O. to "Walhallah", 19, Devon Crescent, N.7.'

Iris had sent the postal order, with a short note asking for a
reading, and a week later had received a reply. She thought of
it now, and searched in a drawer for the typewritten letter; when
she found it, she sat on the bed and read it again, although she
almost knew it by heart. This is what she read.

'Dear Miss Metcalfe,
Many thanks for letter and enclosure. Have carefully
psychometrised your handwriting and cast your horoscope.
A reading follows.
I should say you are of a highly inspirational tendency,
surely sensitive and a bit nervy – liable to take offence and fly
off the handle – resentful of interference, all up in the air –
surely you seek expression artistically? In song or acting, no
doubt have a talent for woodcuts, needlework, crochet or
some such. Of a peculiarly sunny temperament – always
merry and bright – should consort with others of cheery dis-
position, or folks out of the common – how shall I say? – a bit
bohemian.
Marriage indicated not far off – should meet fiancé before
Whitsun next – older man, grey hair, I should say of the
"distingué" type. Offspring are indicated – you love the
kiddies and are a great favourite with them.

86

Oh, I get a whiff of sea air – would you be intending a holiday on the East Coast? I get a ginger gentleman much in your thoughts – oh, he does laugh a lot!

Message from the Other Side – get the name Muriel – do not despair – all will right itself – do not ponder your troubles but continue on the daily round with trust in Him who watches over you constantly – let your heart be high and sing "Rock of Ages Cleft for Me".

God bless you, dearie, and cheerio.

Marianne Robinson-Williams (Mme.)'

On first reading this letter Iris had been disappointed, recognising little in it that applied to her situation; but now she wondered whether she could identify the ginger gentleman with Mr Hill. Mr Hill was not, it is true, ginger, but he had sandy hair, and he had certainly laughed a lot about Devizes.

'Much in my thoughts . . . Well,' Iris thought, 'if that really is Mr Hill, there is no reason why all the rest, the grey-haired man and so on, should not come true.' She felt consoled by the letter, as she had not done till now, and put it back in the drawer with a feeling of mild excitement.

She heard the front door close, and moved quickly to the window where she watched Mr Hill, swinging his pork-pie hat, walk jauntily, and, it seemed to her, self-consciously, as though he knew she was watching him, down the garden path, and along Buckingham Road. She would have liked to have called out 'Goodbye', to him, and even opened her mouth to do so, but no words came, and she recognised the wish as one of many, which made up her life, and which she knew would for ever remain unfulfilled.

She stared out past the common at the sordid houses on the outskirts of Norford. Behind them round, irregular gasometers stood against the sky, and even further away, out in the country, a skeleton viaduct crested a hill. She watched a toy express creep along it noiselessly, bound for the Cornish Riviera, and wondered if the travellers, from the carriage windows, could notice the white speck which was her window in 'Kalipur'. One day she would take that train, and sit in a corner seat to see if her house was visible.

She heard her mother's heavy footsteps on the stairs. Ashamed of being discovered idling – for there was a chance that Mrs

Metcalfe was coming into her room – Iris quickly left the window, and pretended to hunt in a drawer for something. Mrs Metcalfe did come into the room. She sat down on the bed, breathing heavily and fingering her ear-rings.

'Well,' she said, staring at her daughter's back, 'what became of you?'

'How do you mean?'

'I don't know what that poor youngster will think of you. You never said goodbye to him.'

'He wouldn't have noticed.'

'No, very likely he wouldn't. But, dear, you might have been more civil at tea. Weren't you feeling well?'

'I've got a headache. I came up to lie down.'

'I don't know why you don't pull yourself together when we have company. Not that it makes any difference to me. I speak for your own good, dear. But when I asked this young man to tea, I thought to myself, "Perhaps he will do as a friend for Iris". You don't have many friends, you know, dear.'

'I have all the friends I want.'

'Meaning that silly Miriam?' The mother shrugged her shoulders. 'Well, that's your affair. Far be it from me to interfere. But all the same I see no reason why you should bury your nose in your cup, mumble into your beard, and run from the room like a frightened schoolgirl. You can never hope to be happy if you . . .'

'I'm perfectly happy.'

'How can one be happy without friends? Look at me. Apart from you, dear, and Alan, I live for my friends now. And Alan, he was never any trouble, he was always a good mixer.'

'I don't want many friends, Mummy.'

'How can you hope to get married if you haven't any friends?'

'Oh, leave me alone.'

'No dear, when I see you mess up your life by your manner, which isn't the real you at all, I feel bound to correct you.'

'Well, what do you want me to do? Run up and kiss every man I meet?'

'Don't be cheap, Iris.'

'I'm quite all right, all I ask is to be let alone. There's a lot you don't know about me . . .'

'I suppose you mean,' said Mrs Metcalfe sarcastically, 'that you have some dark secret in your life, some great romance, eh?'

'What if I do?'

'No, my dear, that's too childish, there isn't much that gets past me.'

'Very well,' said Iris, 'if you prefer to think that . . .'

Iris left this sentence unfinished, and saw that she had disturbed her mother, who said, with eyebrows raised, 'I've always made a confidante of you, and I've naturally supposed that you tell me everything.'

'Don't let's talk about it any more. I've got a headache.'

'You want to be left alone with your secret, I suppose.'

'Yes.'

But Iris realised that her mother would never rest until she had found out for certain, either what the secret was, or that it did not exist. She foresaw an 'atmosphere' at dinner; a silence broken only by loud sipping of soup in the dining-room; pursed lips over knitting in the drawing-room after the meal.

'No,' she said, 'I haven't a secret romance. So you needn't worry about that.'

Mrs Metcalfe relaxed. 'Well, why the devil did you lead me to believe . . .? Oh, you're impossible! I can't say a few words in my own house without all this hullabaloo.'

'There wasn't any hullabaloo.'

'My dear, we're two lonely women, that's what we are, not as young as we were, and if we're going to quarrel when we're alone, God knows how we'll end up. Come on, my pet, kiss and make up.'

Iris kissed her coldly on the forehead. Mrs Metcalfe patted her shoulder, and chuckled.

'Well, all I can say is, thank God for my sense of humour. I don't know what I'd do without it. I've got a few chores to do before the shops shut, so I'll leave you with your headache. I'll be going to Smith's. What do you want out of the library?'

'See if they've got the latest Warwick Deeping.'

When Mrs Metcalfe had gone, Iris returned to the window. She thought defiantly, 'There *is* something she doesn't know about. She doesn't know about the letter, and the grey-haired man. She doesn't know about that, and she never will.'

She saw her mother leave the house, carrying a leather shopping bag. Mrs Metcalfe moved slowly, waddling slightly as she walked. Some children, who had been playing on the common, paused in their game to watch her. When she started down Buckingham Road, one of them, a little boy wearing a big cap, with a button on the top of it, walked a few yards behind her, imitating her gait with exaggerated gestures, while the other children did not conceal their giggles. Iris could not bear to see her mother made ridiculous, and she moved away from the window.

Saturday

THE town was so full on Saturday afternoon that the only place to have tea was at the café of the Elektra cinema. Its gold walls were decorated with pictures of film stars, all taken some time ago. From behind a door which led to the Circle inside the cinema the programme could be heard playing itself out fatalistically; it was the penultimate performance of the week.

The girl at the cash desk was reading a green Penguin book called *Mr Fortune, Please*. She was supposed to supply a loud radiogram beside her with records, for the amusement of the people taking tea at the café, but she had lazily adjusted it at Repeat, and an old recording of 'Rio Rita' played itself again and again, with a whining noise at the beginning. She found it easier to concentrate on her book to the accompaniment of one tune which she knew and liked, than to a disturbing variety which might distract her thoughts.

The six customers were served by an old waitress in a girlish uniform, who wore a green bow in her yellow hair. She brought the little girl and her governess, who had sat for a long time silent, a pot of tea and some assorted pastries. The child, whose name was Mary, wished that she were watching the film, having never seen real people on the screen, only Snow White and the Seven Dwarfs. A cat jumped on to the chair beside her, and she said affectedly and carefully to her governess, 'O! Look at the pretty pussy.'

Miss Hunt began to eat with a faraway look in her grey eyes. She had had a busy day shopping, and this moment was her first of relaxation. In ten minutes the crowded bus which she had to catch was going to leave from outside the cinema; she would really have liked to be watching the film herself, but she could not have taken her pupil. It was raining outside; Miss Hunt's purchases were heavy.

91

Two nuns, in their loose black clothes, with wicked spectacled faces, were also in the restaurant. They spoke to each other softly, and looked about them with sharp eyes. One was heard to say to the other in a high voice, '. . . it appears she went into the dining-room, ate the apple, and left the core on the side-board . . .' A man in a blue overall came through the curtained door from the cinema, and disappeared through another marked 'Private'.

A small soldier with very large eyes which gave him a sad appearance sat at a table, his heavy equipment beside him on the floor, eating the one-and-threepenny tea which he had ordered some time ago. This consisted of a pot of tea, beans on toast, and two slices of bread and margarine. He had been travelling all day, and still heard in his brain the bored voice of the girl who had announced the name of this station again and again through a megaphone as the train stopped. He was only in the town for an hour or two, and had that evening to continue his journey. Mary was staring at him with serious eyes, imagining herself giving up her seat to him in a railway carriage, because he was a soldier.

The soldier noticed at the next table to his a very tall girl; she wore no stockings, and the rain had made her ankles red. She tucked her hair delicately under her helmet-like hat with great strong hands which made the soldier imagine her capable of murder. Her face, too, had the hard, blurred look that one sees in newspaper photographs of murderesses at their trials; one imagined her covering it with a black sleeve to avoid the photographer's flare. Unconscious of what the soldier was thinking, but conscious of his presence, she took off her glasses which the steam from her tea had clouded, and with a sigh and a movement in her chair began to clean them with a strip of cloth provided for that purpose.

Miss Hunt took from her bag a letter from her brother, who was a missionary in Africa, and began to read it, after wiping round her pursed mouth with the handkerchief which she kept in her cuff. 'Mustn't read at table,' said Mary in a gay tone, but seeing that her pleasantry fell flat she adjusted her face to a serious expression and began to eat her éclair slowly with the oddly-shaped fork by her plate. Miss Hunt's brother had all the fascination for her of the unknown relation. That evening, when, tired and uncomfortable, she ate her supper of sodden cereals at the nursery table, Miss Hunt, she knew, would unscrew her fountain-pen, take the writing-pad mysteriously called 'Hieratica Bond' from the dresser drawer, and answer her brother's letter with compressed lips. The sound of a shriek came from the cinema, a maddening irritation to the little girl's curiosity, and the nuns left the room, having paid their bill at the cash desk, an imaginary crocodile of schoolgirls trooping behind them.

Somehow a conversation had arisen between the tall girl and the soldier; he was showing her his snapshots. 'This is my young lady,' he said, and she adjusted her glasses to look at a moon-faced, smiling girl, in a dress that reached to just above her ankles. 'I wanted her to have a Polyfoto, but it was too dear.' His sad eyes seemed to ask her to listen to him, because he had spoken to no one all day, and she leant forward on her sharp elbows with a smile on her face, while her fingers began to pull and pinch at her neck, and to lift her string of beads to her mouth, and to rub it nervously against her dry lips. The soldier then offered her a Player's Weight, and after fiddling unsuccess-fully for a time with his lighter, he lit their cigarettes. She smoked hers too fast, and half of it was soon a hard burning stretch of tobacco, not yet turned to ash.

Her tea finished, Mary opened and shut the small bag on her lap with gloved fingers. She had enjoyed her day in the drizzling town, avoiding the swirling gutters, spent in the huge draper's shop where the children were amused by someone dressed as Santa Claus and a Hornby train running furiously round and round a table, and in the crowded parlour of Miss Hunt's bearded friend who kept a school for typing and short-hand – the sound of typewriters in the next room, and the smell of the sweat of women, a smell which Miss Hunt knew well and accepted as part of her life. The child was sorry that the day was nearly over, for she looked upon it as a rare glimpse into the mysterious world inhabited by Miss Hunt and her kind – a world which was illustrated for Mary by the odd, old-fashioned advertisements which she sometimes saw on buses and at railway stations. Well-known phrases, such as 'Mazawattee Tea', 'Pullars of Perth', 'Peak Frean', seemed to have no meaning other than a secret one comprehensible only to Miss Hunt. She looked carefully at her governess who sat like an image in her blue tailor-made suit and white-satin blouse; both were dreading the journey home in the bus. They knew from experience that they would be unable to sit down until almost at their country destination, when it was dark outside and every passenger but themselves had left the bus. They had that long stop to face at a village three miles from theirs where the moon shone on a white pool. Last of all there was the walk uphill from the bus stop to the house. Mary's stitch and Miss Hunt's headache solidified in the heavy Christmas parcels which they would be carrying. Mary knew that, as always after a tiring day, it would seem to her as she entered the house by the back way that she was seeing the familiar sight that she saw with dazzled eyes indoors under a different aspect, as the first impression of a place later to become well-known subtly differs from the one that is afterwards given and remembered.

Two women came into the café talking about the film.

'It's a dual role,' said one, 'she plays herself and her twin sister.'

'Yes, a psychological picture,' said the other.

Miss Hunt rose to pay her bill with a frown.

'It must be the end of the first house,' she said, but Mary could not think what she meant by this, and did not like to ask her.

As they left the room, the soldier went up to them with a parcel which Mary had left on her chair.

'You've forgotten this, Missy.' She said, 'O, thank you,' with a coy expression, and followed her governess who had not seen this incident.

In the Ladies' Cloakroom Miss Hunt spat on her handkerchief and rubbed it hard against her pupil's cheek, after tying Mary's sou'wester under her chin with a painful jerk. While she was doing this, the tall woman came in, and Miss Hunt bustled out, as though ashamed, or unwilling to let the little girl see this intruder. Alone in the cloakroom, the woman took off her hat and shook her hair away from her face. After washing her hands vigorously with the small strip of soap that remained, she looked with interest into the mirror above the basin. Beneath the glazed windows of the lavatory the six o'clock bus left with Miss Hunt and her parcels swaying inside it; the news began on the wireless in the restaurant, and in the cinema the organist, a fat little man in evening dress, spun up from underground in a mauve spotlight and bowed to the audience who clapped kindly. He then began to play old tunes whose words were projected on to the screen so that the audience could sing them. The girl

94

looked at her own face in the glass because she had forgotten what she looked like; and she felt that she still did not know, that the reflection in the mirror had as little meaning to her as her own name when too often repeated. She went back to the café, and was surprised to find the soldier still there.

'It's nearly time for my train,' he said. 'Would you care to walk with me to the station?'

He was suddenly sorry to leave this town which had at first seemed so dreary.

They left the café together.

The Visitor

'ADAM and Eve and Pinchme went down to the river to bathe; if Adam and Eve were drowned, who do you think was saved?'

'Pinchmenot!' shouted Mary.

'If frozen water's iced water, what is frozen ink?' Susan asked patiently.

'I stink,' said Mary, and then covered her face with her hands while her friend danced round her, screaming with triumph.

'Don't make so much noise,' called Miss Hunt, who was sitting on a garden seat a short way off, her work basket beside her. She was cutting out some brown paper patterns, with the ultimate aim of providing herself with a dress for the following summer much like the one she was now wearing. Its sleeves came to just above her elbows, its skirt to just below her knees; its neck was V-shaped, displaying a patch of her sun-burnt, freckled skin. Her hands busy with the scissors, Miss Hunt lifted her gentle eyes to watch the little girls playing on the sunny lawn at the back of the house.

Susan's fair hair had been cut short, and only covered half of her ears, so that the back of her neck had a naked look. Her stout body was shrouded in a tunic-like dress too big for her; her small eyes hidden by steel-rimmed glasses, respectful consideration of which prevented her games with Mary from becoming too rough. Susan's shrill voice irritated Miss Hunt, who liked her least of her pupil's friends, and who was usually in a bad humour when Susan had been asked to tea.

Mary's knickers were made of the same material as her dress. Her thick, well-brushed hair hung below her shoulders; her large serious eyes implied a criticism of everything they saw. She was easily shocked, easily surprised, and easily impressed. She now stood on her hands, and for the fascinating moment before she fell over saw the house and her governess upside down.

Miss Hunt hurried towards her. 'Now you've ruined that frock,' she said.

Mary rose from the ground with dignity, staring with reproving eyes at the little patch of green which remained on her skirt. Susan, who knew that the whole performance had been for her benefit, watched in silence.

'It will soon come off,' said Mary.

At this moment a servant came out of the house and said to Miss Hunt with pointed lack of ceremony, 'Miss Mary's wanted in the drawing-room.'

'Run along then,' said Miss Hunt. 'You would choose that moment to fall over, wouldn't you? O dear, O dear, O dear.'

When Mary had followed the maid indoors, Susan sat on the garden seat, but all her attempts at conversation were snubbed by the governess's monosyllabic replies.

Mary knew that her mother had a visitor in the drawing-room; she had seen him arrive, in uniform and on a motor-bicycle, from the nursery window. She knocked with confidence at the door.

'Come in, darling,' called Mrs Stone.

Mary waited for a few seconds, and then opened the door a short way and squeezed through it. She shut it carefully, and remained with her hands on the knob.

'Come and say how-do-you-do, darling. You mustn't be shy,' said Mrs Stone in a voice which she took care to make natural. She was a pretty woman of thirty; her hair was arranged in curls at the top of her head. She smiled at her guest, an officer, who was sitting in a low chair with a whisky and soda on the ground beside him.

'Hullo, Mary,' he said.

Mary came slowly over to him and shook his hand, staring at him fascinated. He was embarrassed by her stare, and tried to make a joke of it by holding her hand for an unnecessarily long time.

'Come and sit by me on the sofa,' said Mrs Stone.

Mary obeyed, still staring at her mother's friend.

'Tell Tim what you've been doing today.'

All Mary's poise now left her. Suddenly shy, she wriggled her shoulders and squirmed on the sofa, digging her chin into her neck but still looking solemnly at Tim.

'You've got a little friend to tea, haven't you?'

'Yes,' said Mary in a low voice, overcoming a longing to turn her back on both the others and hide her face in the sofa.

'I know a trick which will make you laugh,' said the young man. He took an enormous white handkerchief from his pocket and wound it round his hand, making it look like some animal.

'I can do that,' said Mary in a voice which her acute and involuntary shyness filled with meaning.

'I bet you can't,' said Tim. 'Come over here and do it then.'

Her timing as subtle as an actress's, Mary went up to him and snatched the handkerchief from him.

'Don't stare at poor Tim so, darling,' said Mrs Stone. They watched the child in silence while she fumbled slowly with the handkerchief, breathing loudly. At last she threw it on the ground. 'I can't do it,' she said, smiling.

'Don't you like that handkerchief?' asked the man.

'Silly old handkerchief.'

Tim put his arm round Mary's waist and lifted her on to the arm of his chair.

'Don't encourage her to be silly,' said Mrs Stone.

'Won't you tell me what you've been doing today?' asked the young man, looking up at Mary's face.

She could no longer look at his, but without answering stared down at his chest, and began to fiddle with a button on his tunic.

'That button's very bright, isn't it?' he said. She continued to finger it, slowly smiling. 'I bet you couldn't polish it so bright.' She again wriggled her shoulders, and began to swing her legs, unfortunately knocking over his whisky and soda with her foot.

'Here, steady on,' said Tim, while Mrs Stone said crossly, 'O, look what you've done.'

'O,' said Mary, and covered her face with her hands.

'It doesn't matter, darling,' said her mother quickly, 'the glass isn't broken.'

Tim wiped up the spilt drink with his large handkerchief.

Mary pressed her hands hard against her face to stop herself from crying with shame.

'Give yourself another drink, Tim,' said Mrs Stone. 'Perhaps you'd better go back to Miss Hunt now, darling.'

'Goodbye, Mary,' said Tim, syphoning soda water into his

glass. 'Don't go kicking over anything else now.' He clumsily tapped her under the chin.

'Goodbye,' said Mary.

She went out of the room looking at the ground, her hands behind her back, kicking out her feet in a careless way. She waited for a short time silently in the hall, hoping to overhear her mother or the officer say something about her. She had sometimes heard Mrs Stone say to a guest, 'Isn't she sweet?' after one of these short visits. She now heard them talk of other things, however, so she walked back thoughtfully to Susan and Miss Hunt.

Going to School

JAMES and Mary Stone were to start school on the same day. Mary, who was nine years old, was going to a place called Field House, which was only twenty miles from her home; James, aged eight, to a well-known preparatory school fifty miles away. At first it had been arranged that Mr Stone should drive James here, and perhaps have a chat with Captain Jennings, the headmaster, before he left, while Mary and her mother travelled by train to the girls' school, where Mrs Stone might have a word with Matron; but James had cried so loudly, and had threatened so convincingly to throw himself from the window of the lavatory in which he had locked himself unless *he* was accompanied by his mother, that the plan had been reversed. So now Mr Stone and Mary sat opposite each other, alone in a dirty railway carriage with old photographs of bathers on the walls and thick china mugs containing brown remnants of tea under the seats. The train had no corridor, and stopped at even the smallest stations on their journey; sometimes it stopped in open country, for no reason at all. Mary was more assured than her father, who had dressed smartly for the occasion; he wore a dark suit, an Old Harrovian tie and a black Homburg hat. Mary wore a coat and skirt from Debenham and Freebody's and a hat to match pulled well down over her thick hair. She carried a bag which contained a comb, a mirror, and half a crown. She smiled politely at her father all the time, but he saw that she was nervous when she began to fidget, and to trace a profile on the misted window-pane beside her.

'I shouldn't do that, Mary, it's rather dirty.'

'Why?' she asked with curious eyes; then noticed that the finger of her woollen glove was stained. She effaced the drawing with her sleeve, and sat silent, thinking about her friend, Susan. They had had an emotional parting scene that morning, and had exchanged locks of hair. Susan was to go to another school, one exclusively for clergymen's daughters. Mary had slipped the thin, straw-coloured, straight bit of her friend's hair, tied by a blue ribbon, into her sponge bag which was now in the suitcase on the rack above her head. Mary sighed, and said for the second time, 'I wonder how Mummy and James are.'

'Yes, I wonder,' said her father. He lit a cigarette, removed a piece of tobacco from his lip, and looked out of the window, whistling softly. Both were conscious of something unsatisfactory about this journey; perhaps it was the fact that all the other girls were arriving on a later train from Paddington, and Mary knew that she would have to wait an hour at the station before driving with them to the school in a special charabanc. As these girls left the train, Mr Stone was to board it, and thus be transported back to his home station.

'Perhaps,' said Mary, 'it would be nice if I did take an Extra.'

'I thought you'd decided against it.'

'I might wait and see if all the other girls do.'

'Which would it be, Mary? Painting, music or dancing?'

She thought for a moment, then said, 'Dancing.'

'You'll only be able to dance with the other girls, you know.'

'Yes, of course. There won't be any boys at school.'

'But won't that be poor fun?'

'No, Father.' She laughed, and said conversationally, 'I wonder if all the other girls will be bigger than me? Miss Hunt used to tell me I was tiny for my age. Poor Miss Hunt, she was very sad to go away.'

'I expect there will be some your size,' said Mr Stone, remembering the day when the governess had left sobbing in a taxi, and Mary, after one hour of depression, had been surprisingly 'good about it'.

'I wonder if the mistresses are decent. Miss Gough sounded awfully sweet on the phone. I wonder if I shall have a friend.'

'Won't it be fun when your best friend comes to stay with us in the hols?' said Mr Stone cleverly.

A new expression came to Mary's face. 'Yes, won't it? And won't it be fun when my report comes?'

'And mind it's a good one, my girl.'

Mary squirmed in her seat. 'Buck up, old train,' she said.

When they arrived, they found the station small and deserted, built two miles from the town at the end of a lane. As the train left them standing on the platform with Mary's trunk and suit-case, they noticed two big piles of luggage, one at each end of the station. They reverently examined the labels on one pile; the girls of Field House must have sent their trunks on in advance, all instinctively doing the same, and apparently the right thing. Mary read out the names on the labels in an awed voice.

'Muriel Clive, Heather Poole, Hazel Poole – they must be sisters – Shirley Hollis, Felicity Thorpe-Nicholson, crumbs, what a name!'

The other pile belonged to Greengates, a rival school, hated by Field House. 'They come back tomorrow, but they broke up a week after we did,' said Mary, who had this knowledge from a mysterious source and was speaking as though already of the school. A charabanc with 'Private' written on the front, empty but for the driver, jogged up the lane and stopped outside the station. The driver got out and stretched himself. Mary dis-covered a slot-machine under an advertisement for Brylcreem, and tried to work it with a penny borrowed from her father.

'O blow, it's bust,' she said, 'and I would so so like a Mintip.'

It was cold on the platform, and the girl clapped her hands and shook them up and down, trying to get warm. Mr Stone began to feel apprehensive, at the same time longing for and dreading the arrival of the train with the other girls on it. He was filled with affection for Mary, who ran up and down the roofless bridge over the line, living entirely for the moment. He thought sympathetically of his wife, who was probably having a difficult time with James, and said to himself with pride, 'It's going very well. We get on together, Mary and I.'

They went for a walk in the fields – for there was nowhere to have tea – and picked blackberries from the hedges. Later, the driver of the charabanc called to them, 'She's signalled.' Mr Stone glanced nervously at Mary, who took hold of his hand, and then immediately let it go. She had a concentrated expression on her face; her eyes stared as though just not weeping; she was sucking her under-lip, and all the time moving from one foot to the other. Her father was thinking, 'It will soon be over now'; he was thinking of himself, not of her. The train came into the station.

Several very tall girls stepped out, all surprisingly mature; one, Mr Stone noticed, was almost attractive. They fussed shrilly over their smart suitcases; many had brought golf clubs. A small woman, evidently a mistress, came up to Mary, glanced at Mr Stone, and told Mary, 'You must be Mary Stone.'

A girl with long fair plaits and big breasts who was passing said, 'That's the new bug.'

Mary grasped the mistress's hand; her father had never before seen her so ill at ease. She looked much smaller than the other girls, and altogether different.

The mistress said, 'Stay with me, dear,' and hurried off to talk to the driver.

Mr Stone climbed into the train, which gave no sign of leaving. He felt like an unwanted guest at a picnic; the girls ignored him, but Mary attracted some casual attention as she dumbly followed the mistress. The others talked to each other in a bullying way. 'O, don't be flabby!' they said, or 'O, don't be mouldy!' Mr Stone wondered if Mary would return after thirteen weeks using these unpleasant expressions.

The guard waved his flag. Mary said calmly to the mistress, 'Excuse me, please, I must say goodbye to my father.' She ran to the window of his carriage. 'Goodbye, darling,' he said, leaning out, 'the best of luck. Write and tell us how you get on. Be brave.' She could only look at him with agony suddenly in her eyes. She was frightened. He again said, with less conviction, 'Be brave.'

Mary seemed to want to fling herself into the carriage, into safety. The train began to leave the station with slow, silent jerks. Mr Stone wondered whether or not to kiss her; then decided that it might embarrass her. He saw her turn away with an angry face, and, listless and self-conscious, join the other girls who at first ignored her and then surrounded her with brutal curiosity as the train took him away.

*

Mrs Stone drove the grey Ford V8 through the flat country interlaced with tumbledown stone walls. Her son sat stiffly beside her, clutching his copy of *The Modern Boy* with clammy hands. His hair, cut short, jutted out in ridges; his eyes swam behind bent steel-rimmed spectacles; the straps of his knickerbockers hurt below his knees. Both he and his mother felt sick with dread. To whatever she said, he answered nervously, 'Yes, but . . .'

'Father and I are coming after three weeks. Captain Jennings said that was the earliest we could. Now, that isn't very long, is it, old boy?'

'Yes, but . . .' What he meant to say was, 'It is ages.'

Every now and then pretty Mrs Stone had to stop the car so that James could relieve himself behind a hedge. 'What will happen,' he said, suddenly desperate, as he climbed back into the warm car, 'if I want to do that in class?'

'I suppose you'll ask the master, and he'll let you go.'

'But suppose he won't let me?'

'Of course he will. Masters are quite kind, darling.'

'Father said they weren't.'

'Schools were different when he was a boy.' Mrs Stone was praying to God, 'Make it go off all right. Make him not cry.' But James was thinking, 'I wish the car would crash, and I was killed. No, not killed, but very badly hurt, and taken to hospital in an ambulance, and fussed over.' For the last few days, while his trunk was being packed and name-tapes being sewn on his clothes (his school number was 73, the lowest in the school), he had hoped to die before being delivered into the terrible unknown, and had several times thought of suicide; but he had always realised in time that there were left a few days, or hours in which the catastrophe for which he prayed might happen; an earthquake might swallow up the school, killing the Jenningses and all the masters.

'Look, there's an aerodrome,' said Mrs Stone. James would not look at it, but murmured, 'That means we must be nearly there.' An aeroplane flew low over their heads as they turned a corner, and saw the grey solid school-house standing beyond stretches of playing-fields with skeleton goal-posts and a wooden pavilion. This was James's last moment; thirteen weeks was for ever, too long to wait before resuming a life which, although not appreciated at the time, now seemed Heaven. His mother had told him often that the school was more like a private house than a school; he saw now that this was not true. It might have reminded other boys of their homes, but to James it was obviously an institution, for even at a distance it lacked the luxurious air of a hotel. He clasped his mother's tweed sleeve and said, 'Stop the car.'

'James,' she said sharply.

'Stop the car,' he said impatiently. The school had not been burnt to the ground as he had hoped; he was determined to go no nearer to it. 'I'm not going on,' he said, his voice shaking. He reached for the brake but Mrs Stone anticipated him, and the car stopped.

'Now, darling, you promised to be brave. Think how good Mary was, I'm sure she isn't making all this fuss.' Two cars passed them, driven by furred mothers and containing red-capped sons with round, beaming faces. Mrs Stone said desperately, 'Don't cry, James. For my sake.'

He was crying hopelessly, turned away from her. 'I'm not going. I can't bear it, I shall die.'

She whispered, 'Be a man. It's as bad for me as it is for you, darling, really it is. Here, use my hanky.'

He said, 'It's all *right* for you. You've at least got Father, but I shan't have anyone at all.'

'But everyone has to go to school.'

'I don't have to.'

'And you'll see me in three weeks.'

'I can't wait three weeks.' He said more calmly, 'You must come next Sunday.'

Mrs Stone remembered the headmaster's suspicious words: 'You know, we don't allow them to be taken out for the first three weeks. They must have time to settle down. Parents are sometimes very unreasonable.' She said uncertainly, 'Will you go bravely if I promise?'

James turned towards her. 'You must swear,' he said, threateningly.

'I promise, darling.'

James shut his eyes and leant back, as he had done when at last persuaded to take the dentist's anaesthetic. His mother started the car again, feeling that by diplomacy she had saved her life. They turned up the drive, shaken by emotion and left almost comatose.

The house *did* have a deceptive appearance of being like any other house; but behind this façade, in which the Jenningses themselves lived, the school buildings were as drab as a prison. The boys and their parents were received in comfortable surroundings, but the children never saw these again; and after those first three weeks, so subtly calculated by Captain Jennings, hypnotised by school life they could only tell relieved mothers and proud fathers that they had enjoyed themselves. They came back for the holidays changed; their masters, impelled by an instinctive hatred of home and parents, had alienated them for ever from their natural backgrounds. This was to happen to James, but not until after weeks of suffering.

Parents and children were leaving their grand cars as though arriving at a party. The Jenningses stood on the porch; the Captain in plus-fours, with thick black eyebrows and moustache; his wife with frizzy fair hair, no eyebrows and face and hands heavily powdered. Near them a master, dressed in a baggy grey flannel suit, was moving about, smiling nervously. This was Mr Clarke, who had been shell-shocked in 1915 and made uneasy, effeminate gestures with his arms.

'How beautifully punctual you are, Mrs Stone,' said Mrs Jennings, laughing. They had met at race meetings. She patted James's head as he stood with his feet apart, red in the face and furious. 'Would you like to talk to Matron about James – or Stone as I ought to say now, oughtn't I? Some boys take Glucose, or Radio-Malt or things.'

'No, thank you, I don't think James needs anything.'

'I see you are going to be an ideal parent,' said Captain Jennings jovially, but with a hint at menace, as though saying, 'Don't you dare be a fussy mother.' He hit James's round shoulders. 'Well, Stone, have you ever played football?'

Appalled at her son's silence, Mrs Stone heard herself say, 'Yes, he has played rugger with friends, haven't you?'

'Splendid,' said Captain Jennings, and turned away. His wife said, 'We play soccer here, but he'll soon learn.'

Other parents were leaving now, after kissing their children in a jolly way. Mr Clarke called out in a strange, high voice, 'Follow me, boys!'

'He'd better go to tea now,' said Mrs Jennings. 'Do you want to see the dormitories?' She whispered, 'It's wiser to leave them as soon as you can,' making an understanding grimace.

James said, 'I've had tea.'

'Run along, darling,' said Mrs Stone, 'I must go now if I want to be home before dark.' She bent to kiss him, but he did not kiss her, just saying loudly, 'Remember. Sunday.' Mrs Jennings, watching, pretended not to have heard this and said, 'The cat has got his tongue. I should follow the others, dear.'

James went off, skipping with false nonchalance, and disappeared round the corner of the house with Mr Clarke and some chattering boys who were also hiding their apprehension by an assumed assurance. Two of them were fighting each other behind the master's back, and one cried out 'Pax!' in a touchingly childish voice.

Mrs Stone did not watch him go. As she climbed into her car, dreading the lonely journey home, Captain Jennings came up to her, and said carelessly, 'You know our rule about three weeks, Mrs Stone?' She felt that he resented her being a woman and a mother, and began, 'I was just going to ask you if . . .' Before she could finish he said firmly, but pleasantly, 'We can never alter it, you know.'

'But if he is ill?'

'We have a sickroom, and the Matron is a trained nurse.'

She remembered, on her first visit to the school, a glimpse of the sickroom and clean, pyjamaed boys sitting up and drawing in bed.

'I see,' she said.

She could think of no more to say, and decided to consult her husband about her promise to James. She wondered sadly what her child was doing, how he was feeling, whether or not he could see her as she drove away from some strange window.

*

That evening, the house seemed unnaturally quiet. 'It's lonely without them, isn't it?' she said to her husband at dinner.

'I suppose we'll get used to it in time. Mary was marvellously plucky.'

'James was very upset, but I think he was all right when I left him.'

'Poor little chap. Did you speak to Captain Jennings?'

'Yes, he seemed quite nice.'

'I didn't see Miss Gough, thank God. These women terrify me.'

They were silent. Mr Stone was thinking, 'This is what it will be like when they are grown up, and have left home.' Mrs Stone was thinking of what James had said: 'You at least have Father, but I shan't have anyone at all.'

The Facts of Life

THROUGH the big bow window of Captain Jennings's study he could see the skeleton goal-posts on the football field deserted now in summer, and beyond them the flimsy bungalow which two of the junior masters shared. Low grey stone walls intersected the flat country; not far off there were pine trees. When he turned from the window back into the room, it seemed to him that the green leather on the chairs was sweating in the heat, that backs of his books on the shelves were melting, and that Vermeer's 'Girl with Ear-ring', reproduced over his mantelpiece, had turned paler and drooped in her frame more than usual. It was the last day of term. Captain Jennings placed one large foot on his desk; then leant his elbow on his knee and his chin on his hand, while his other hand plunged and fidgeted in the pocket of his grey flannel trousers.

He was always embarrassed by these end-of-term talks with the leaving boys. All had gone well so far this afternoon; there now remained one more boy to see. Newton had not fitted in at Greenfields. Never bullied, he had at the same time never been popular with master or boy; indifferent both at games and work, he was yet by no means a dud; from the age of nine his unattractive face had suggested to Captain Jennings a wizened and disturbing sophistication unsuitable in a boy and impossible exactly to define. Captain Jennings's lips were moving beneath his thick black moustache in an automatic rehearsal of the scene he was about to act with Newton. When he heard a feeble knock on his door, he said 'Come in' rather louder and more abruptly than had been his intention.

Newton slid into the room, and as had done the other boys this afternoon, took an unnecessarily long time shutting the door behind him. He finally turned a blank, pallid face towards the master, and stood motionless, to attention, with an evident desire to impress which had an irritating effect.

'Oh, er, take a pew, old boy,' muttered Captain Jennings.

'Thank you, sir.' Newton sat down slowly.

'I'd like to have a little chat with you before we say goodbye tomorrow. Man to man, you understand, nothing in the nature of a lecture.'

'Yes, sir.'

The boy seemed bored. Captain Jennings went on, putting expression into his words, but not enough to make them sound spontaneous.

'This is always rather a sad occasion – at any rate Mrs Jennings and myself find it so – but of course for you it is a milestone in your life. Probably the first important one. How well I remember the last day at my own prepper!' He laughed. 'I had one of those funny lumps in the throat, you know the sort, that get you here.' Captain Jennings touched his collar. 'Silly, but there it was. Couldn't help it.'

'Yes, sir.'

'Nothing to be ashamed of, after all.'

'No, sir.'

'I've got a feeling – mind you, I may be wrong – but I've a feeling that, taken all in all, you've been fairly happy here at Greenfields?'

'Oh, yes, sir.'

'Yes.' Captain Jennings's manner now changed; perhaps he was perplexed by Newton's over-phlegmatic replies. He continued gruffly: 'I know there is an idea going about the school that these last talks I have with the leaving boys are nothing but pi-jaws about sex. I shouldn't like you to run away with that idea. The fact is, once you chaps have reached this, er, stage in your life, I feel you need a few words of friendly advice. Of course you don't have to take it if you don't want to. I don't know how much you discuss with your own people – that's none of my business. You must realise that your life up till now has been rather, well, sheltered. I mean you've had a lot done for you here at Greenfields, and if you've made any little mistakes, they won't have had any serious consequences. But once you get to your public school, you'll be in a position to make or mar your whole future life yourself. Before I send you out into the world, as it were, there are a few little points I'd like to clear up with you. Do you compree so far?'

'Yes, sir.' Newton turned his attention from the window back to the schoolmaster.

'Now I'm sure you've got a few questions you'd like to ask me, Newton. Anything that's puzzled you, or bothered you in any way.'

'No, sir, I don't think so.'

'You don't have to feel embarrassed with me, you know. I mean, about sex, and all that rot.' There was a silence. 'I know, among fellows your age,' continued Captain Jennings, 'there's a good deal of rather futile giggling on that subject, smutty little jokes, and so on. Oh, I don't mean this personally, Newton; I've no idea what you've been told at home, and it's none of my business. But I am very keen to impress upon you that that particular attitude is really rather silly and childish. I know love sometimes seems awfully sloppy – at the cinema, for instance – often want to be sick myself when I go to the pictures. Nobody hates sentimentality more than I do. But I want you to realise, all ragging apart, that love can, and should, be a wonderful thing, a beautiful thing.'

'Yes, sir.'

Captain Jennings did not look at the boy; he seemed now to be talking to himself.

'The great thing is to look upon it in a healthy way. That is the key word – health. As long as you keep fit, you see things in their true proportion. I know some aspects of life can be pretty foul, but there's no reason you should ever have to bother your head over that, as long as you keep a healthy mind in a healthy body. I forget whether you have a sister, Newton?'

'No, sir, I haven't.'

'Well, we all have mothers, and if we want to be worthy of the name of gentlemen, we should think of women, and the love of man for woman, with the deepest respect.'

'Yes, sir.'

Captain Jennings coughed loudly, and the boy looked away self-consciously.

'When you get to your public school – Radley, isn't it? – there are a few things I want you to bear in mind. Choose your friends among the boys of your own age – there's bound to be some good fellows among them. If an older boy tries to pal up with you, don't pay any attention. And of course, when you get older yourself, you won't want to run around with any of the younger fellows. Oh, and it's always better that you don't make friends outside your own house. You must remember that a public school is said to be the world in miniature. You'll probably come into contact with a certain amount of tommy-rot while you're there, but you must remember that some boys won't have had your advantages, and you must pity them without having anything to do with them. Don't ever be afraid of sneaking if you stumble across anything you know to be wrong. You know that thing that goes, "I am the captain of my fate, the something of my soul" or something? Kipling, wasn't it, or one of those johnnies? I always think it's rather appropriate.'

'Yes, sir.'

'Yes.' There was another silence. Captain Jennings frowned down at his feet; Newton fidgeted in his chair, an expression of polite interest on his face. The master suddenly went on: 'I don't know what your people have planned for you later on, but it's possible that you'll go to the 'Varsity, as I did myself. You may find that a certain type of older woman will try to get hold of you. You don't want to get involved with anything like that.'

'No, sir.'

Captain Jennings looked at Newton, as if taking him in for the first time. The boy looked young for his thirteen years. 'Mind you, it's early days yet to be thinking of anything like that. But when the time comes, remember my advice, Newton; steer clear of older women. I don't want to depress you. After all, we're all part of Nature, when you come to think of it, and Nature can have her beautiful side. I mean, it's really pretty marvellous to think of a tree growing, and flowers, and even animals . . .' Captain Jennings's voice died away, as it met no response in his pupil. He began again: 'If you're lucky, when you've passed twenty, you'll meet a young lady in your own set, of about your own age, just as I met Mrs Jennings . . . And then, when you're in a position to think about getting married – but no doubt I've said enough.'

'Yes, sir.'

'You've got plenty of good times ahead of you yet. Games, comradeship . . . Certain there's nothing further you want to ask me?'

'I think that's all, sir.'

'Capital, capital.' Captain Jennings held out his hand. 'Good-bye, Newton, and Godspeed. Enjoy the holidays.'

'Thank you very much, sir. I hope you do too.'

'And drop me a line now and again. We'll send on the mag. Keep in touch, you know. We shall always be interested to hear of your doings. Goodbye, old boy.'

'Goodbye, sir.' Newton slipped his hand from the master's grip, and walked out of the study with the air of performing a difficult feat.

Captain Jennings stood still for some minutes, and then he too left the room. Instead of turning right, as the boy had done, down the dim passage that led to the classrooms, he swung open the green baize door to the left of his study. At once he was in a different atmosphere; here in the private part of the house his wife ruled, as he did in the bleak boys' quarters. The hall, a misleading façade designed to give parents the impression that they were leaving their sons in a home-from-home, was bright and fussy; prints were thick on the pale yellow walls, polish gleamed on the parquet. The drawing-room (into which no boy ever penetrated) was today full of flowers; the predominant colours here were pink, mauve and oyster-grey, and the room gave an impression of consisting entirely of satin. Captain Jennings found his wife curled up on a sofa, surrounded by tasselled cushions, reading the *Tatler*, and occasionally helping herself to a marshmallow from a box at her elbow.

Marjorie Jennings wore neither lipstick nor rouge, but her face was covered by thick powder, beneath which her lips thinned and her eyebrows disappeared altogether. Her hands were powdered too, while her frizzy pale hair looked as if it might have been. She smelt strongly of this powder, traces of which she often left behind her on chairs and sofas – a trail of dust. She smiled at him her understanding smile.

'Tired, Porker darling?'

He turned his back to the empty grate, stretching his legs as though he were warming them. 'Nearly finished.'

'I know. And then the nicest holidays of the year. I've written off to Keith Prowse for seats for Leslie Henson.'

This remark of his wife's immediately put Captain Jennings in a better temper. He suddenly longed for the delights of the summer holidays as intensely as any of his pupils. Matinees, race-meetings, garden-parties, picnics . . .

'Are we changing tonight?' asked Marjorie.

'I think so. I asked Fairman to dinner, and I expect he'll put on a black tie. He's made an awfully good start this term, you know. The boys respect him.'

'He did well in the war.'

'Yes, but that's not it. Look at Banks. Wonderful war record, but can't do a thing with his class. All over the shop, all over the shop.'

'We must have a talk about Matron.'

'Yes, darling, but later, later.' He went towards his wife and patted her hand. 'Better see how they're getting on at the nets. I'll see you at prayers.' Marjorie smiled at him again, and then reopened the *Tatler* as he left her.

As Captain Jennings walked in the sun to the cricket field, where Mr Banks was taking fielding practice, he smiled to himself; he had remembered another summer, nearly twenty years ago. He was in his second year at Oxford; Marjorie had been brought to tea in his rooms by her brother, another undergraduate. They had soon discovered that they shared the same ideas on many subjects . . . That night they had met again at a college dance; they found that they liked the same tunes. The next day he had taken her on the river, and they had played the gramophone. What was the name of that song they had both liked so much? He still had the record somewhere. Just by whistling it softly to himself, he could bring back the smell and texture of those days.

As he reached the nets, Captain Jennings remembered the words, and the boys paused in their play, surprised to hear the master suddenly sing out, loud and true,

> 'You're the cream in my coffee,
> You're the salt in my stew.
> You will always be
> My necessity,
> I'd be lost without you.'

Sunday

Doris stood in her slip in her attic room before the small mirror dabbing Odorono on her armpits with a red brush. Too impatient to wait for it to dry, she tugged over her head a cotton dress and then pulled it down over her body catching her nose in the neck of the dress which wrinkled over her hips and stretched tight across her breasts. Her slip still showed beneath so she adjusted it clumsily at the shoulder-straps with two golden safety pins which she had been holding in her dry lips. She combed out her frizzy orange hair so that it stuck out in a solid mass behind her head like a veil in the wind, and then she squeezed her broad feet into a pair of high strapless shoes, of a wine colour to go with her dress. She had fat hairless legs and arms, but a slight red down could be seen from below on her upper lip. Her pig eyes looked lost without their glasses which she wore as seldom as possible. She felt in her bag to see that all its contents were safe; a white square inch of handker-chief, a flapjack with her lover's powdered photograph over the mirror, a ten shilling note four times folded and a crumpled Penguin book, as yet unread.

Red-faced Daphne awaited her in the porch, asleep in her perambulator. The muscles of her white limbs bulging with the strain the maid pushed the child up the dusty hill, closed and deserted on Sunday afternoon, and Daphne opened her eyes to look complacently at Doris's big face on which the sweat began to clot the yellow powder. Doris saw her auntie in brown as always at the window over the bookshop and lank-haired Muriel who worked there with her boy, a rating. 'Going to the pictures tonight?' 'Not on a day like this, it would be a crime.'

A lorryload of whistling soldiers passed slowly and Doris thought, that's a nice feller, the young one. She looked the other way as she passed the place where she knew was chalked on a red brick wall a vulgar drawing of Old Man Hitler, and by it had been for a long time the slogan Mosley Will Win, now methodically crossed out but not erased. Doris began to whistle, her mouth pursed to a mauve button, and thought, now what's that I'm whistling, it's been on my brain since Friday, and, silly, I can't call to mind its name. If I forget about it it will come to me suddenly, in the night or while I'm working, the name of it.

Daphne agitated her wrinkled arms in a worried and impotent way but Doris, who disliked her, took no notice. They reached the common high above the town and Doris sat on an empty seat and pushed the perambulator slowly up and down before her with her hand, so that the brown fringed hood hid Daphne from her sight. Behind her small boys and girls played cricket on the grass; a shock-haired schoolmaster headed a troop of red-capped boys out on a walk, shouting to them in a high voice now and then. Doris looked down the road at the town beneath her; she saw the house of her employers alone and squat by the black canal which crossed the town, and near it the yellow silent houseboat moored to the path by the lock. From where she sat the railway station was like a toy sold in the shops before the war with Hornby trains. It was a little way out of the town and now a short train shunted slowly backwards and forwards, sending out white smoke to evaporate in the fields and the cemetery near by. For ten minutes Doris thought about nothing.

Her brain said to her, Here comes Fred. He wore a bright blue suit and was whistling, that tune her brain had been singing since Friday so now she said to herself, of course, The Whistler's Mother-in-Law.

'Hullo, Fred.'

This was not her day off, Wednesday, so her manner was strained. She made room for him on the seat uneasily because she did not want to make herself common like Muriel, on the common. She laughed at her private pun.

Silent Fred and she looked together now at the town, and her hand left the perambulator to rest in his. They noticed the gasworks in the slums of the town where they sometimes walked on her day off. Thinking of this she remembered girls in shabby dresses of bright colours too big for them who played complicated games with balls on the narrow pavements and did not make room for them to pass. A madwoman had croaked at them from an open doorway.

Fred's hair was shaved at the back as if he were in the Forces. Sometimes Doris wished that he was, but she knew that she had a lot to be grateful for. As he lived in the same town he had never had occasion to write her a letter, which she would have enjoyed in some ways more than his company; she thought of the letters girls had shown her written in blue ink on lined YMCA notepaper.

Fred worked in a bank and was not in the army because of his weak chest. He had a kind face with a worried expression, broad hips and small hands and feet. Doris's flashy way of dressing and painting seemed to bid for a more exciting fellow, but she was so ugly that she could be content with Fred. To him her frizzy hair, small eyes and tight white smile were pretty. Her hand which clasped his was threaded with soapy white lines, marks left by continual washing-up. It smelled of soap and her close-cut nails were dirty. Fred's hand was clean and manicured, and on one hairy finger he wore a ring. His creased shiny black shoes were no bigger than Doris's beside them, resting on the grass as though still in the shop beneath her naked blue-veined legs.

A child ran under the seat on which they were sitting and then away, frightened. Doris was thirsty. Daphne grimaced in her perambulator and howled for a time with desperate choking sobs. Fred and Doris sat together all the afternoon, their hips touching and her hand in Fred's on his crumpled blue serge lap.

Later the inhabitants of the town left their houses after resting, all at the same time, and climbed the hill sweating and gasping to queue outside the cinema on the common which opened late because it was Sunday. They wanted to escape from the heat outside into the stuffy, more restful atmosphere of the cinema where they could rest on velvet seats and stare wide-eyed at a flickering screen instead of with screwed-up eyes at dazzling colour and haze.

A party of girls in the ATS came laughing up the hill singing 'Bless 'Em All', led by a small stout woman with a pretty face powdered brown who sang in a loud high voice. They jerked their thumbs at passing cars but the cars ignored them, passing them with insulting acceleration while the small woman paused in her song to shout abuse at the drivers. A car did at last stop for them in front of the seat where Fred and Doris sat. Its driver, a bald man, said 'I've only room for four'. There were six girls.

'You go on, Titch,' they all said to the small one who was evidently a favourite.

'You get in, girls,' she answered. 'Me and my friend'll wait for the next one.'

'Buck up,' said the driver, who was wasting his petrol. Four climbed into the car and drove off in lower spirits leaving behind Titch and her friend who was tall and had a big pale face and shingled hair. The friend caught sight of Daphne.

'O, isn't he a duck?' she said. 'Come over here, Titch, isn't he a duck?' She looked at Fred. 'And isn't he like his Dad too?'

Titch crossed the road and looked inside the perambulator.

'It's a girl,' said Doris with a consciously sweet expression and a slight frown.

'I bet you're ever so proud of her. What's her name?'

'Daphne.'

Daphne stared at them placidly. The two women looked at her for a time in admiring silence, and then Titch said, 'Come on, Lofty, we must be on our way.' They walked off with swinging strides like men.

'They thought she was our little girl,' said Doris after a moment's silence.

'Perhaps we will have a kid some day,' said Fred. 'When we're married.'

'O, don't be wet,' said Doris uncomfortably.

A dark aeroplane passed low over their heads, and on the ground its shadow moved quickly over the common. In the town Doris's auntie walked slowly with some other women to the evening service in the church opposite the town hall outside which there was a notice advertising a dance on Wednesday, Alberto and his Mexican Mandoliers. A slight breeze caught the hood of Daphne's perambulator like a sail, and it began to roll down the hill unguided, with Doris's bag and the child in it as placid as before. Doris screamed, 'O, the pram,' and dumb Fred ran after it, his red tie flapping over his shoulder while Doris stumbled behind him. They ran some way down the hill after the pram, which moved madly, faster and faster until finally Fred caught up with it and stopped its progress, and Fred and Doris looked at each other panting and sweating, horrified at their adventure. Doris began to giggle guiltily and Daphne to bellow, realising late that something unsual had happened to her.

That evening Doris changed into a dark green dress and stuck a white cap on her head. The sun shone through the laurel-shaded windows of the dining-room on the pale faces of Daphne's mother, Mrs Hollis, and Mrs Hollis's mother, Mrs Redman. With flushed face and suspended breath Doris removed the dirty plates from under their greedy mouths. They ignored her creaking shoes and the rustle of her dress when it stretched under her arms. Mrs Hollis ate her soup, cold meat and beet-root, and fruit salad with her mouth open and when she spoke her mother saw the food as a white mass behind her teeth. Mrs Redman was a large woman of slow movements. She ate with compressed lips and dared not speak for fear of betraying the wind in her voice. A fat black spaniel sat under the table, old and dying. There were yellow stains on the ceiling; the house was damp, as it was on the canal. Mrs Hollis said:

'Molly Homes heard from Cecil again last week, Mother, did I tell you? And her brother has been mentioned in des-patches, they think. Remind me tomorrow to take Hester to the vet. Doris, has Hester had her dinner?'

'Yes.'

Mrs Hollis chuckled to herself. 'Sybil's expecting hers next month. Well, I hope it will be all right. It's the third time she's tried.'

Mrs Redman lifted her eyebrows in a silent question and her daughter formed answering words with her mouth without uttering them. '*Pas devant*,' she said, and Mrs Redman nodded wisely.

Mrs Hollis had tied up her hair neatly with a blue chiffon scarf and painted brown stockings on her legs. She touched her ear-rings in a distracted way, crossed her legs and lit a cigarette which she took from a pocket over her breast, screwing up her eyes as she did so and blowing the smoke out of her mouth and upwards by putting her lower lip outside her upper lip. This did not suit her as her teeth protruded slightly. She said:

'I went up to speak to one of the Italian prisoners working at Chapman's and the guard came up and said I wasn't allowed to. They seemed quite civil fellows. The Eyeteyes. I saw a little winter frock in Mason's window might do for Shirley. It was rather a pet, dear, but I should say worth the money.'

She yawned widely, making an unpleasant moaning sound at the back of her throat.

After dinner Doris went upstairs to turn down Mrs Hollis's bed. She could hear the wireless in the drawing-room play a selection from *The Student Prince*. She laid out the satin pyjamas which had the initials P.H. worked over a breast pocket. Then she critically inspected Mrs Hollis's make-up on the dressing-table, smearing her wrist with alternative samples of lipstick. Doris noticed a letter on the dressing-table, which she instinctively picked up and read.

'My dearest Priscilla (otherwise known as Poppet),

By the time this reaches you I shall have arrived at where I am going. The voyage has been pleasant, but excruciatingly dull. There is a bloke on board I knew at school – Gerry Baker. I share a cabin with him and two other Majors, which is jolly. There is little to do but drink – and there is plenty of that, thank the Lord – and play cards, so as you can imagine we are all impatient to arrive and get cracking! I am also impatient for your first letter, my sweet, telling me how you are and all the gang. Gerry Baker has two daughters the same age as Shirley and Daphne which is a coincidence, isn't it? How are the little beauties, bless their hearts? Give them their daddy's love, if they remember him. I doubt if little Daphne will remember me when I return. How are Shirley's teeth?

Everyone on board is very sanguine about the war ending soon. I hope to God they are right. Jerry's going to get a kick in the pants he isn't expecting. Well, I know my little wife is keeping her chin up. The days are grey, but it won't be for long. And we both have happy memories, haven't we, to last us till we're together again? I know that I have.

I have no news to tell you, so I suppose I had better close now. Cheerio, old lady – and keep smiling.

With love from your devoted

Henry.'

There was a postscript to this letter which had been crossed out by the censor.

Doris then went into Mrs Redman's room. She put ready the old lady's night-dress which was kept in a fluffy case disguised as a rabbit beneath the many pillows on the bed, some pink mules of a dainty colour and design but a large size and a black dressing gown with green dragons painted over it. The room was full of photographs, and on the table were some back numbers of *The Times* and four novels from the Times Book Club. Doris opened a drawer in the hope of finding a letter to read but discovered something much more interesting – a box of Black Magic chocolates which Mrs Redman must have been storing for some time.

The maid knew at once that she must steal them. The sweets would give her much more pleasure than anything could possibly give Mrs Redman. She undid the bodice of her dress and hid the box under her bosom; when she fastened again the hooks and eyes it stayed there firm. She walked calmly up to her attic and placed the chocolates in the bottom drawer of a large chest of drawers recently put there, beside an old copy of *Picturegoer* which had a picture of Irene Dunne on the cover.

That night, dressed in her white woollen pyjamas and sitting on her narrow bed, Doris opened the box of Black Magic and delightedly examined the little map on top of the chocolates which she had not seen for over a year. She picked out a Praline Paté, the chocolate which she knew she liked the least, and ate it, first sucking off the chocolate coating and then crunching the centre. After this she had to eat the whole lot.

Everyone in the house was now in bed. She heard outside in the street the noise of men coming out of the public houses which were closing. Doris pulled on her pink-flannel dressing-gown, embroidered at the sleeves and pockets with twisted white cord and tassels, and clutching the cardboard remains of her theft hurried downstairs to the kitchen. She burnt the empty box in the dying fire, stirring the embers with the crooked poker which she used so much in the daytime. A fat black beetle ran over her naked foot.

Back in bed Doris felt very sick. The night was hot and she pushed the bedclothes off her ill-made bed and lay almost naked, shaking and happy in wait for the sleep which she knew would come.

The Dancing Lesson

THE soldier climbed the stairs to the top of the house, his heavy boots clattering on the stone. He stopped outside a door which had a green curtain drawn across it; on it was written, 'The Adair School of Ballroom Dancing. Private Lessons any Time.' There was also a photograph of a man and a smiling woman dancing together, holding each other at arms' length. From behind the door came the sound of Victor Sylvester's band playing 'Amapola'. The soldier went into the room, a large bleak studio with a skylight on which the evening rain was spattering. There were green chairs along the walls, a big clock and a gramophone near the door. In the middle of the room a girl and an Air Force officer were turning slowly, holding each other, and occasionally eyeing their reflection in the mirror on the wall. They ignored the newcomer who sat down and watched them.

The record came to an end, and the girl broke away from her partner, leaving him alone in the middle of the room, and went to the gramophone. She was small and thin, with black hair and a sharp, pretty face which she had powdered very white. She wore a tight black dress, a white artificial flower pinned to her shoulder, and high-heeled silver shoes. She said to the officer, who was now changing his shoes, 'When would you care to come again?' She recorded his answer in a book by the gramophone, and turned her attention to the soldier. He had arranged a course of lessons that morning, and as he had only a short time for them, she had offered to give him that day half an hour after the time when she normally closed the studio.

'Have you done any dancing before?'

'No.'

'We had better start with the quick-step, which is the simplest. Aren't you going to change your shoes?'

'I haven't brought any others.'

The girl frowned, and started 'Amapola'. He found it difficult to dance with her, because she was so much smaller than him. At first he was conscious of an amused audience in the last pupil, who soon left, after wishing the girl 'Good Evening'. She punctuated the lesson with instructions given in a bored voice: 'One, two, three, and slide; one, two, three, and over; no, the left foot, not the right . . .' He felt humiliated when because of a mistake he had made they stopped, and had to start again. Her head came to his chest; his hand was hot on her thin shoulder-blades, and she pulled away from him with an almost vicious determination, her small legs moving automatically, followed by his clumsy, khaki ones. Often his boot trod on her toes, and although he apologised, she did not answer. Together they slid the round of the room, and then she put the same record on the gramophone again.

There soon arose a sense of hostility between them. He was too shy to laugh at his mistakes, and she made him realise, by an air of aggravated misery and bitter pathos, that but for him she would be now walking to her home, her tiring day of work finished. He felt both irritated by her, for she made him feel clumsy, and sorry for her, because she did look really ill. He could hardly bear to see their ridiculous reflection in the mirror, alone in the big room while the rain hit the glass above them, because it suggested that he was unwillingly torturing this conscientious little woman, who did not complain. The clock clicked after every minute, and he looked at it so often that the hands seemed to move unusually slowly.

His nervousness ended in disaster. A brutal stamp on her silver shoes unbalanced the teacher, and with an incredible loss of dignity she fell to the floor, and stayed there, her head turned away. He knelt down to help her up, and saw that she was crying. She said nothing, but made no effort to rise, and he guessed that she had hurt her ankle, and was waiting for the pain to subside. After miserable apologies, he said, 'Let me help you to a chair and it will soon pass off,' and put his arm round her thin shoulders. To his surprise, she yielded to his support; he sat down on his heels, and her head fell back on his shoulder, so that she looked up at him with sharp, weeping eyes. She had for him all the agonised pathos of smallness, and for a moment he wanted to hurt her more. He saw now that there were lines

on her face, and noticed a white thread in her hair. He put his
other arm round her, the rough khaki chafing the skin on her
bony arms, and she began to cry more desperately, the cry of a
child which follows the pause after sudden pain. Not embarrassed
any more, he held her in his arms, uncomfortable on the hard
floor, mirrored impersonally on the wall. Her head was pressed
against his shoulder, her hollow throat against his chest, while he
stared down at her neatly arranged hair, at the straight white
parting which divided her head. Her nails, with their 'Natural'
polish, were digging at his back, as one clenches one's hand to
overcome the sense of pain. But it appeared that she had not
sprained her ankle after all, for she rose slowly after the clock
had clicked a minute, pulled down her dress, and went to the
gramophone where she took a handkerchief from a black bag
with silver clips. She blew her nose and dabbed at her face. The
soldier's feet were numb, and he rose heavily. The record had
come to an end.

'I'm sorry,' he said again.

She shut up her bag and looked at the clock. 'When would
it suit you to come next?'

He helped her pull a cord which drew a blind across the skylight; together they fastened the door, and as they walked downstairs he rehearsed in his mind the suggestion to be made at the
bottom that he should see her home; find out her name, and
perhaps take her to the cinema in the evenings when they were
both free.

The Town

THERE are certain parts of the town where a grey depression awaits the lonely traveller. One of these is the station buffet. It is to this sad place that he first goes, tired and hungry, on his arrival.

The door from the station to the buffet, which has the letters, 'Refreshments', cut from the dark blackout paper pasted on its glass so that at night the dim light from the room shines through and forms the word, is often stuck and discouragingly hard to open; inside there is a smell of sour tea and stale paste sandwiches. Tables are attached to the tiled floor. Behind the wet sloping counter a fat girl with huge white legs, wearing a black silk dress which hangs low in front and is hitched up over her behind, sells with a resentful air these sandwiches, hard as stone and piled up like a card castle beneath a glass dome. When asked for tea she pours a little off-white milk into a cracked china mug, indifferently washed and left to dry itself; then she adds an inch of tea which she draws from a steaming urn, and fills the cup with boiling water from another. She suspiciously slides in a few grains of sugar, and then stirs the mixture with a stained spoon tied by a piece of string to the ornate till, which is itself fastened to the counter. The tea tastes only of its heat and what sugar there is in it, and when it has been drunk a sediment of brown powder remains at the bottom of the mug. Along the wall behind the counter are wine-bottles containing coloured liquid and crisp empty cigarette cartons – all advertisements of non-existent wares. When there are any cigarettes, they are sold loose, and some slip from the waitress's fingers on to the counter, where they become sodden and are ruined. The clock has stopped at ten past ten, and its glass case is ajar.

Sometimes the waitress has a friend with her behind the counter, and then she can continue while serving with a story which she has been telling in instalments for several days. 'She didn't say anything to me at the *time* – no coffee, only tea. Beer the other end of the counter,' she says, although there is no one but herself to serve the beer at the other end of the counter, for her friend is obviously not expected to help her even when she is very busy. At a slack moment, bringing her hand down to squash an insect crawling up the till, she might tell a favoured customer, 'You know I couldn't keep from laughing this morning, when I came here I saw a big grey rat on the counter, big as that he was. He must have been at the sandwiches.' Then, over her shoulder, she replies in a softer voice to her friend's question, 'Ah, but that would be telling, wouldn't it?'

Mingling with the noise of the trains outside can be heard the polite, mysteriously ubiquitous voice of the woman who, apparently perched somewhere on the station roof, announces their departure and arrival, and tells passengers to 'hurry along to the bay, please, your train is waiting.' One of the workmen who comes to the buffet every morning before catching the six-thirty, wrapped in scarves and blowing on their hands, to buy a cup of tea from the waitress whose eyes are still sticky with sleep, is in love with the owner of the voice, and as he has never seen her imagines her to look like Dorothy Lamour.

In the evening the place is filled with the women porters who come in at eight o'clock laughing and joking for some beer. These are the only customers with whom the waitress is friendly; to any others she says, 'Haven't you anything smaller?', or 'Have you the extra halfpenny?', in a bored and offended voice which is meant to dissociate herself from her surroundings, and implies that all the time she is thinking of the glamorous life which she leads when away from the station. She knows that she sees people at a disadvantage, when they are fussed and apprehensive, and this gives her a low opinion of human life.

Outside the trains shriek and sigh. Tired women sit at the tables, luggage and children piled about them, sipping their tea – for drinking tea is often the most satisfactory physical experience that their lives can offer them. Its heat calms their nerves and its very tastelessness is comforting. Parting couples make stumbling conversation in the buffet, saying the same thing again and again but never admitting that they are longing for the train to arrive, and the parting to be over. They clutch at the present with an avidity that leaves them dumb and senseless. An enormous woman porter, twice the size of any of her male associates, leans over the bar and says grandly, 'I'll have twenty Woodies, Rita, and give me a pint.'

'Mild or bitter?' the waitress asks coyly.

'Either, so long as it's wet,' says the porter, and some people in the buffet laugh. The air gets thicker, and Rita more and more dazed and sick. Soon she will stumble home in her mackintosh, through the wet streets, to the soft bed that awaits her in a house by the railway line – for she does not escape the noise of trains even at night. Soon, also, it will be six o'clock; time for her to wash in a basin beneath a naked bulb, dress and return to the buffet where someone will be swilling the floor, muttering to herself. The days pass quickly and happily for Rita, and by now she does not notice the smell of tea and the noise of the trains; they have been absorbed by her senses, and she would only notice their absence.

Another place where life seems to be at its lowest ebb is the lending library over the booksellers in the High Street. The books that line the walls have all been rebound by the library in brown covers, and their titles are printed in illegible gold lettering. Cardboard bookmarkers, covered with mysterious pencil marks, dangle from their backs. The more pencil marks that a book has on its cardboard extension, the more popular it proves itself to be. Only the newest books, available to a few subscribers who pay more than the others, have no markers, and sometimes have not yet been rebound so that they look more readable than the older, uniform volumes. These have been arranged in alphabetical order on the shelves by the single assistant, Miss Fraser, who is a small woman with frizzy pale hair and spectacles that look as if they hurt her. In summer the sun glitters on the backs of the novels as though it might melt them; there is a smell of leather in the library and Miss Fraser sits wilting in the stuffy room behind a desk on which she has placed a jar of flowers as limp as herself. Sometimes she is busy knitting bedsocks for herself with painfully thin steel needles; sometimes she sits idle, staring through the large bay window at the street, dabbing at her sharp nose with a small handkerchief which she keeps secured to her knee by the elastic strap of her knickers, and which therefore smells faintly of underclothes. At teatime she takes some bread and butter wrapped in tissue paper from the pocket of her check coat which hangs with her hat (either a pixie hood or a rabbi's cap) behind the door, and munches it slowly while crumbs fall between the pages of the books which she handles. Her fountain-pen has left two inky bumps on her middle and forefingers.

All day Miss Fraser's customers, who are mostly ladies in light-brown fur coats who live in the northern suburb of the town, stump up the broad staircase from the shop and fish their books from net shopping-bags, either with a reproachful air because they have not enjoyed their choice, or with patronising commendation because they have. They speak in low voices, as though at an oracle; and Miss Fraser is the goddess of the oracle, for they take it for granted that she has read every book in the library. 'Would I like this?' one might ask, doubtfully deciphering the title of a novel. 'I want something light but not trashy.' Miss Fraser answers with a frown, 'It's not as good as his others,' or, defiantly, 'Well, *I* liked it,' but she never gives away the fact that she does not read novels, or indeed anything, as reading makes her head ache, and that she is only interested in playing tennis, and tennis champions. She can tell, however, from a glance at a book, which of her customers it will please; and she can even successfully supply with amusement ladies whom she has never seen, invalids who do not leave their houses, but send out companions to Miss Fraser with long instructions written in spidery handwriting on scraps of paper. The librarian is conscious of her responsibility towards these, and sends them the new Warwick Deeping or Cecil Roberts with the air of a doctor prescribing a tonic wine. There is but one male subscriber, a Mr Young, who never asks Miss Fraser's advice, and is always wanting books that she has never heard of, or that are out of print; he seems to have joined the library owing to some mistake, and she respects him more than any other of her customers.

Miss Fraser despises readers of books, but rather admires the writers, for she thinks that they must be clever, not because they write anything of value, but because they can write at all. She knows how important it is for a novel to be long, and the longer a book is the more she admires its author for the purely physical feat of writing down so many words on so much paper. Miss Fraser feels that she conspires with the writers to dupe the readers and so her attitude to the latter is a mixture of contempt and apology. The ladies who visit her day after day respect her and are fond of her, but she pities them and if one of them asked her to tea on Thursday she would not go. To please them, and to help business, she sometimes volunteers a scrap of information about her private life, so that a customer can ask while changing a book, 'How is your sister who was so poorly at Easter?' or 'Have you heard again from your brother in Kenya?' With instinctive art she exactly limits the extent of her personal relationship with the readers – she would always nod if surprised by one off duty at the Kardomah Café or buying slides at Marks and Spencers – but privately she classes herself apart from them, with the unseen writers, on a higher plane, the practiser of a fraud, the exploiter of the vice of reading.

As a young girl, Miss Fraser had wanted more than anything else to be another Betty Nuthall or Helen Wills Moody. Now, on summer Thursdays, she is able to change into a pleated white dress and stroll with her girl friend to the public courts, each balancing a box of balls marked Slazenger on their rackets which are screwed into triangular presses. She plays well; on these afternoons she is energetic, her face has a colour, and even her hair seems alive, but for the rest of the week she must wilt in her hot-house, her eyes dim, a sneer stamped on her face. 'What they really need here,' she thinks sadly, 'is a girl who is fond of reading', but she dare not leave her job as she might never find another. By now, however, she has come to think herself lucky to be able to do what she wants for a few hours every summer week.

Just as in the station buffet it is the depression caused by squalor that assails one, and in the lending library that of vegetable refinement, so in the Tudor Bar of the town's most expensive hotel does there come a moment when silence falls, time stops and the atmosphere is stale.

High, steel, immovable stools sit up at a streamlined bar. Until recently the room has been picturesque, as indicated by the name it still bears, but now it is modernised and gives the impression of an angular design in red and white. Small flamboyant girls, with hair sometimes an inky blue, sometimes a decorative pink or a dazzling yellow, but always piled high above their heads as though supported by a hidden construction of wire and cardboard, amuse their escorts in the RAF with a sullen gaiety. The barmaid appears to have powdered not only her face a dusty yellow, but also her hair and hands, and even her clothes and the Parma Violets sagging at her bosom. Every drink except for rum has run out, and its sickly smell fastens on the room and the people in it like hair oil on a plastered head.

Sometimes a husband and wife who are staying at the hotel penetrate into the bar, looking about them defiantly and moving self-consciously – for usually the residents look upon the bar as out of bounds, preferring to have their drinks brought to them by a waiter as they sit in one of the lounges. There, however, there is little to do but turn the pages of the *Morris Owner* until that magazine assumes a sickening familiarity; and as neither member of a married couple owes the other the politeness of conversation, towards the end of the evening boredom drives them into the bar. The woman immediately sits down, while the man sidles furtively up to the bar itself, now and then turning round to signal to his wife, who may ignore his signs, or answer them with a restrained nod. Eventually he returns balancing the glasses, carefully pushing them ahead of him through the crowd, and for the rest of the evening they sit and sip together, not looking at each other, unable to hide a feeling of superiority, and convinced that any remark they might make will be as embarrassingly audible to everyone in the noisy, smoky bar, as it would have been in the soporific, silent lounge where they really belong.

Just as a drunken bonhomie can suddenly change into a testy, quarrelsome misery, so the atmosphere in the bar, as the evening progresses, becomes less and less gay and careless, more and more bitter and hostile. Quarrels start between lovers, and between men who have never seen each other before. The barmaid has dark shadows under her eyes, and as the drink runs out appears to think that she is being blamed. The married couple want to go to bed, but each feels that if he or she suggests this, the other will be offended and the evening will be ruined. Only the red-faced drunk, who is found leaning on the bar each night, is happy and smiling, because he is now in a world where every face he sees, every word he happens to hear, assumes an exciting air of mystery; his brain is drowning and distressing reason has disappeared. Suddenly one of the lights is switched off; an airman shouts, a girl giggles, and everyone feels relieved. The fun has stopped, and the more enjoyable period of looking back on, thinking about and discussing that fun is beginning.

When you leave the bar at closing time, there is nothing to do but walk slowly past the lovers at each shop door in the High

Street, down by the canal where cranes and gasometers in the mist caricature human forms, wondering what it would be like to spend the night, not in the bed to which you dread returning, but in the closed and empty Post Office or on the dance floor of the large Town Hall; and to hear the last buses at quarter past ten rock through the silent town, illuminated and sometimes containing ghostly shaking forms, seeming to make more noise than they do in the daytime.